She gazed at him, her eyes soft, and he felt something sparkle to life in his chest as if someone had just plugged in a hundred Christmas trees.

He was falling hard for this lovely woman, who treated his daughter with such kindness.

Fear not.

That little phrase written in his father's hand seemed to leap into his mind.

Fear not.

He was pretty sure this wasn't what his father had meant—or the angels on that first Christmas night, for that matter—but he didn't care. It seemed perfect and right to fearlessly take her mug of cocoa and set it on the side table next to his own, to lean across the space between them, to lower his head, to taste that soft, sweet mouth that had tantalized him all day.

Dear Reader,

In the course of forty-five books, I've written many heroes I have loved: FBI agents, baseball players, police chiefs, vets. Each has moved into a little corner of my heart—and I hope the hearts of my readers. I can honestly say I have never had so much mail from readers about a hero as I have about rancher Ridge Bowman...and I hadn't even written his story yet!

The oldest Bowman brother first appeared as a secondary character in *Christmas in Cold Creek,* published in 2011. With each new Bowman story, more and more readers began asking when I was writing Ridge's book. After Caidy Bowman's book, *A Cold Creek Noel,* came out last Christmas, I quickly realized Caidy's tall, quiet, tough-on-the-outside, soft-on-the-inside brother had already sneaked his way into my readers' collective heart. I began receiving a steady stream of letters, most saying they enjoyed Caidy's book, but *all* asking me when they could read Ridge's story!

I have to tell you, that's a great deal of pressure on an author. I knew I couldn't just create any old heroine for Ridge. She would have to be someone all those readers who already cared about him would deem worthy. I have been delighted with the final results. Sarah Whitmore is kind, smart, caring—exactly what Ridge needs to find true joy at Christmas and always.

All my very best wishes for a wonderful holiday season,

RaeAnne

A Cold Creek Christmas Surprise

―

RaeAnne Thayne

HARLEQUIN® SPECIAL EDITION®

Recycling programs
for this product may
not exist in your area.

ISBN-13: 978-0-373-65781-0

A COLD CREEK CHRISTMAS SURPRISE

Copyright © 2013 by RaeAnne Thayne

Printed in U.S.A.

www.Harlequin.com

RAEANNE THAYNE

finds inspiration in the beautiful northern Utah mountains, where she lives with her husband and three children. Her books have won numerous honors, including RITA® Award nominations from Romance Writers of America and a Career Achievement Award from *RT Book Reviews*. RaeAnne loves to hear from readers and can be contacted through her website, www.raeannethayne.com.

To my wonderful readers. You constantly awe
and inspire me with your passion, loyalty and heart.

Chapter One

The River Bow had never seemed so empty.

Ridge Bowman stomped snow off on the mat as he walked into the mudroom of the ranch house after chores. The clomping thuds of his boots seemed to echo through the big rambling log home he had lived in most of his life, but that was the only sound.

He was used to noise and laughter—to his sister Caidy clanging dishes or singing along to the radio in the kitchen, to his daughter watching television in the family room or talking on the phone to one of her friends, to barking dogs and conversation.

But Caidy was on her honeymoon with Ben Caldwell and Destry had gone to stay with her cousin and best friend, Gabi.

For the first time in longer than he could remember, he had the house completely to himself.

He didn't much like it.

He slipped out of his boots and walked into the kitchen. A couple of barks reminded him he wasn't completely alone. He was dogsitting for Ben's cute little pooch, a three-legged Chihuahua mix aptly named Tripod. Most of the dogs at the River Bow slept in the barn and lived outside, even Luke now—Caidy's border collie, who had been injured the Christmas before—but Tri was small and a bit too fragile to hang with the big boys.

The dog cantered into the mudroom and planted his haunches by the door.

"You need to go out? You know you're going to disappear in all that snow out there, right? And by the way, next time let me know before I take off my boots, would you?"

He opened the door and watched the dog hop out with his funny gait to the small area off the sidewalk that Ridge had cleared for him.

Tri obviously didn't like the cold, either. He quickly took care of business then hopped back to Ridge, who stood in the doorway. The dog immediately led the way back toward the kitchen. Ridge followed, his stomach rumbling, wondering what he could scrounge from the leftover wedding food for breakfast. Maybe a couple of Jenna McRaven's spinach quiche bites he liked so much, and there were probably a few of those little ham-and-cheese sandwiches. Ham was close enough to bacon, right?

He managed to add a yogurt and a banana, missing the big, hearty, delicious breakfasts his sister used to fix for him. Fluffy pancakes, crisp bacon, hash browns that were perfectly brown on the outside.

Those days were over now that Caidy was married.

From here out, he would just have to either fend for himself—and Destry—or hire a housekeeper to cook his breakfast. Too bad Ben's housekeeper, Mrs. Michaels, wanted to move back to be near her grandchildren in California.

He was happy for his little sister and the future she was building with Pine Gulch's new veterinarian. She had put her life on hold too long to help Ridge out here at the ranch after Melinda left. At the time—saddled with a baby he didn't know what to do with, right in the middle of trying to rebuild the ranch after his parents' deaths—he had been desperately grateful for her help. Now he was ashamed that he had come to rely on her so much over the years and hadn't tried harder to insist she move out on her own years ago.

She had found her way, though. She and Ben were deeply in love, and Caidy would be a wonderful stepmother to his children, Ava and Jack.

All his siblings were happily married now. He was the last Bowman standing, which was just the way he liked it.

He nibbled on one of Jenna's delicious potato puffs then had to stop for a huge yawn. The obligations of running a ranch didn't mix very well with wedding receptions and dances that ran into the early hours of the morning.

"Is it still a disaster out there, Tri?"

The little dog, curled up in a patch of morning sunlight trickling in from the window, lifted his head and flapped his tail on the kitchen tile, then went back to sleep, oblivious.

Ridge knew from his walk down the stairs that morning that the kitchen was just about the only clean part

of the house right now. Jenna's catering crew had done
a good job in here and had wanted to go to work on the
rest of the house, but he hadn't let them. He had also
had to shove his sisters-in-law out the door at 2:00 a.m.
when they started wandering around with garbage bags.
He loved Becca and Laura dearly, but by then he just
wanted everybody to go before he fell over, knowing he
had to get up in three hours to start his day.

Given the choice between sleep and a pristine house,
he had opted for the former, especially since he knew
damn well that Caidy, ever efficient, had made arrange-
ments for a cleaning crew to come in today to mop up
after the big party.

He grabbed his improvised breakfast and whistled to
Tri, then headed through the party carnage into his office, doing his best to ignore the mess as the dog hopped
along behind him.

Though it was Saturday, Ridge had plenty of work to
catch up on, especially since the past few weeks leading
up to his sister's wedding had been so chaotic. He had
several emails to deal with, a phone call to a cattle broker
he worked with, ranch accounts to reconcile. Finishing
off the last bite-sized ham sandwich on his plate sometime later, he glanced up at the clock and was shocked
to realize two hours had passed.

He frowned. Where was the cleanup crew? He was
positive Caidy had said they would be here at ten, but
it was nearly noon.

As if on cue, the doorbell suddenly rang, and Tri
jumped up, gave one little well-mannered bark and raced
to the front door as fast as his little hoppy, butt-bouncing
gait would take him.

The housecleaners really had their work cut out for

them, he thought as he walked back through the house. He only hoped they could finish the job before midnight.

With Tri waiting eagerly to see what exciting surprise waited on the other side of the door, Ridge opened it.

Instead of the team of efficient-looking workers he expected to find, he found one woman. One small, delicate-looking woman with big blue eyes and a sweep of auburn hair that reminded him of the maple trees down by the creek at the first brush of fall.

She wore jeans and a short black peacoat with a scarf tied in one of those intricate knots women seemed to like.

Overall, he had the impression of fragile loveliness, and he wondered if the scope of the cleanup job would be too much for her. He pushed the thought away. He had to trust that Caidy had hired a reputable company and that she knew what she was doing. He sure as hell didn't want to clean the mess up himself, especially after he had rebuffed everybody else's offers to help.

"Mr. Bowman?"

"Yes."

"Hello. My name is Sarah Whitmore. I'm sorry to…"

He didn't wait for her apology, he just opened the door wider for her. "You're here now. That's the important thing. Come in."

She gazed at him for a moment, her mouth slightly open and an odd expression on delicately pretty features. After a slight pause, she walked inside.

"I thought you were supposed to be here two hours ago."

"I…was?"

The cleaning service must have mixed up the time. While he was usually hard-nosed about punctuality, she appeared so befuddled and a little overwhelmed—probably at the mess confronting her inside the house—that he decided not to sweat it.

"As long as you put in an honest day's work and do what you were hired to do, I don't see why I need to tell the company about this."

"The…company."

With a slight blush staining her cheeks, she gazed around at the muddle of crumbs, discarded napkins, empty champagne bottles. "Wow. What happened here?"

Man, he would have to talk to Caidy about her choice in cleaning services. The woman's bosses really should have filled her in about the particulars of the situation.

"Wedding reception. My sister's, actually. It was after two when the party finally broke up, and since I had ranch chores to deal with early this morning, you can probably tell I just left things as they were."

"It's certainly a mess," she agreed.

"Nothing you can't handle, though, right?"

"Nothing I can't…"

"It's not as bad as it looks," he assured her quickly. He *really* didn't want to clean all this up by himself. "The catering crew took care of the kitchen, so there's nothing to do in there. Just this space, a few of the bedrooms where guests changed clothes and the guest bathrooms here and on the second floor. You should be done in three, four hours, don't you think?

She gazed at him, a little furrow between her brow, her bottom lip tucked between her teeth.

Completely out of nowhere—like a sudden heat wave in January—he had a wild urge to be the one nibbling on that delectable lip.

The urge shocked him to his toes. What the hell was

wrong with him? He hadn't responded like this to a woman in a long, long time but something about her soft, lovely features, the soft eyes and that silky spill of auburn hair sent raw heat pooling in his gut.

He set his jaw, shoving away the inappropriate, wholly unexpected reaction.

"Cleaning supplies are in the closet in the mudroom, which is just off the kitchen back there. You should find everything you need. I'll be in my office or out in the barn if you have any questions," he said, already heading in that direction in his eagerness to get away from her.

He thought the dog would follow him, but Tri seemed more interested in the new arrival. Not that Ridge could blame the dog for a minute.

"But, sir," she called after him, a slight note of panic in her voice. "Mr. Bowman. I'm afraid—"

The phone in his office rang at just that moment, much to his relief. He didn't want to stand here arguing with the woman. She was being paid to do a job, and he wasn't the sort of boss who stood around like a hall monitor, making sure his people did what was expected of them. She could ask any of his ranch workers and they would tell her the same thing.

The phone rang again. "I've got to take this," he said, which wasn't really a lie, as it was probably the hay supplier he'd been trying to reach. "Thank you for doing this. You have no idea what a godsend you are. Let me know if you need anything."

He left her with her mouth slightly ajar and that look of dismay still on her features.

Okay, so he had run away like he was twelve years old at a school dance and the girl he liked had just asked him to take a spin around the floor with her. It was strictly self-preservation.

The last time he had been so instantly tangled up by a woman, he had ended up married to her—and look how delightfully *that* had turned out.

All he could think was that it was a good thing she would only be there for a few hours.

Sarah now understood the definition of the word *dumbfounded.*

After Ridge Bowman—at least she assumed it was Ridge Bowman—hurriedly left her alone with a funny-looking little three-legged dog, Sarah stood motionless in the big, soaring great room of the River Bow ranch house trying to catch her breath and figure out what had just happened.

Okay, this did *not* go the way she had anticipated.

She wasn't sure what she expected, but she certainly had never guessed the man would mistake her for someone else entirely.

She stood with her hands in her pockets, gazing down at the little dog, who was watching her curiously, as if trying to figure out what move she would make next.

"I would love to know the answer to that myself," she said aloud, to which the dog cocked his head and studied her closer.

The cold knot that had lodged under her breastbone a week ago as she stood inside that storage unit seemed to tighten.

She *ought* to chase after the man and explain he had made a mistake. She wasn't from a cleaning crew. She had flown out from California expressly to talk to him

and his siblings, though she would rather have been anywhere else on earth.

She drew in a breath, her nails digging into her palms.
Do it. Move. Tell him.

The annoying voice of her conscience urged her forward in the direction the ruggedly handsome rancher
had gone, but she stood frozen, her attention suddenly
fixed on a wall of framed family pictures, dominated by
a smiling older couple with their arms around each other.

Sarah screwed her eyes closed. When she opened
them, she looked away from the pictures at the great
room, with its trio of oversize sofas and entwined ant-
ler light fixtures.

He really did need help. The house was a disaster.
The wedding of Caidy Bowman must have been quite a
party, at least judging by the disarray left behind.

Why couldn't she help him?

The thought sidled through her. In that brief interaction, she had gained the impression of a hard, uncom-
promising man. She couldn't have said how she was so
certain. If she helped him tame some of the chaos in his
house, he might be more amenable to listening to her
with an open mind.

As a first-grade teacher used to twenty-five six- and
seven-year-old children, she was certainly used to cleaning up messes. This wasn't really all that unmanageable.

Besides that, she wasn't in a particular hurry to chase
after him. If she had her way, she would put off telling
him what she had found in that storage locker as long
as humanly possible.

The truth was, the man terrified her. She hated to
admit it, but it was true. He was just so *big,* a solid six

feet two inches of ranch-hardened muscle, and his features looked etched in granite.

Gorgeous, yes, okay, but completely unapproachable.

He hadn't smiled once during their brief interaction—though she couldn't necessarily blame him for that since he thought she was a tardy cleaning service. She dreaded what he would say when she told him why she had *really* come to the River Bow ranch.

What would it hurt to help the man clean his house for an hour or two? Afterward, they could have a good laugh about the misunderstanding. Who knows? He might even be more favorable to what she had to say.

Okay, good plan.

She tried to tell herself she was only being nice, not being a total wuss. She unbuttoned her coat and hung it on a rack by the door, grateful her extensive wardrobe debate with herself had resulted in simple jeans and a lovely wool sweater. As much as she loved the sweater, wool always made her itch a little so she wore a plain and practical white long-sleeved T-shirt underneath.

She pulled the sweater over her head, rolled up the sleeves of the T-shirt to just below her elbows and headed into the kitchen for the cleaning supplies.

He was right about the kitchen. The big, well-designed space sparkled. She headed into the area she guessed was the mudroom and found an organized space with shelves, cubbies and a convenient bench for taking off boots. A big pair of men's lined boots rested in a pile of melting snow and she picked them up and set them aside before quickly drying the puddle.

She easily found the cleaning supplies stored in one of the cubbies in a convenient plastic tote. She picked the whole thing up and carried it back through the house.

First things first, the clutter of garbage all around, then she could start wiping down surfaces and work on the bathrooms.

As she walked through the big, comfortable great room picking up party detritus, she wondered about the Bowman family.

She knew a little about the family from her initial research, the quick web search she had done after finding that storage unit that had led her to this place and this moment. She had learned a little more after her arrival in Pine Gulch, Idaho last night, thanks to a casual conversation with the young, flirtatious college student working as desk clerk at the Cold Creek Inn where she had stayed the night before.

She knew, for instance, that the charming inn where she stayed was actually owned, coincidentally, by the wife of Taft, one of the Bowman brothers.

From the clerk, she had discovered there were four Bowman siblings. Ridge, the hard, implacable rancher she had just met, was the oldest. Then came twins Taft and Trace, the fire chief and police chief of Pine Gulch, respectively. And finally the daughter, Caidy, the one who had been married the day before—much to the chagrin of the desk clerk, who she quickly deduced had nurtured an ill-fated secret crush on Caidy Bowman, now Caldwell.

The ranch appeared to be a prosperous one. All the buildings were freshly painted, and the big, comfortable log home could easily have doubled as a small hotel itself. It was large enough to host a wedding reception, for heaven's sake.

The Christmas tree alone was spectacular, at least eighteen feet tall and decorated to the hilt with ribbons, garland, glittery ornaments. More evergreen garlands twisted their way up the staircase and adorned the raw wood mantel of the huge river-rock fireplace.

This was more than just a showplace. She could tell. This was a home, well maintained and well loved.

As she headed up the stairs to collect a pile of napkins she could see on a console table in an upper hallway, Sarah had to fight down a little niggle of envy. She couldn't help comparing the splendid River Bow ranch house to the small, cheerless apartments where she had lived with her mother after the divorce.

What child wouldn't have loved growing up here? Sliding down that banister, riding the horses she had seen running through the snow-covered pastures, gazing up at those wild mountains out the wide expanse of windows?

She frowned as she suddenly remembered the rest. A lump rose in her throat.

Oh. Right.

She knew more about Ridge Bowman than how many siblings he had and the outward prosperity of his ranch. She knew he and his brothers and sister had suffered unimaginable tragedy more than a decade earlier, the violent murder of their parents in a home-invasion robbery.

She could only guess how the tragedy must still haunt them all.

That ever-present anxiety gnawed at her stomach again, as it had since she walked into that storage unit, and she pressed a hand there.

She had to tell him. She couldn't keep stalling. She had come all the way from Southern California, for heaven's sake. This was ridiculous.

With fresh determination, she gripped the now-bulging garbage bag and started down the stairs.

She wasn't quite sure what happened next. Perhaps her heel caught on the edge of a stair or the garbage bag interfered with her usual balance. Either way, she somehow missed the second stop down.

She teetered for a moment and cried out, instinctively dropping the bag as she reached for the banister, but her hand closed around air and she lost what remained of her precarious balance.

Down she tumbled, hitting a hip, an elbow, her head—and finally landing at the bottom with a sickening crunch of bone as her arm twisted beneath her.

Chapter Two

At the first hoarse cry and muffled thud from the distant reaches of the house, Ridge shoved back his chair so hard it slid on the wood floor a few inches. He recognized a sound of pain when he heard it.

What the hell?

He jumped up and raced out of his office. The instant he entered the great room, he found a slight form crumpled at the bottom of the stairs, a bag of garbage spilling out next to her and Tripod anxiously whining and licking her face.

"Go on, Tri. Back up, buddy."

The little dog reluctantly hopped away, allowing Ridge to crouch down beside the woman. Her eyes were closed, and her arm was twisted beneath her in a way he knew couldn't be right.

What was her name again? Sarah something. Whitmore. That was it. "Sarah? Ms. Whitmore? Hey. Come on, now. Wake up."

She moaned but didn't open her eyes. As he took a closer look at that arm, he swore under his breath. Maybe it was better if she *didn't* wake up. When she did, that broken arm would hurt like hell.

He had known a couple of broken arms in his day and had enjoyed none of them.

The woman had appeared fragile and delicate when she showed up at his house, too delicate to properly handle the job of cleaning up the wedding mess by herself. Now she looked positively waiflike, with all color washed from her features and long brown lashes fanning over those high cheekbones. Already, he could see a bruise forming on her cheek and a bump sprouting above her temple.

He looked up the stairs, noticing a few pieces of garbage strewn almost at the very top. Must have been one hell of a fall.

All his protective instincts urged him to let her hang out in never-never land, where she was safe from the pain. He didn't want to be the cause of more, but he knew he had to wake her. She really needed to be conscious so he could assess her symptoms.

A guy couldn't grow up on a busy Idaho ranch without understanding a little about first aid. Broken arms, abrasions, contusions, lacerations. He'd had them all—and what he hadn't suffered, the twins or Caidy had experienced. Judging by her lingering unconsciousness, he was guessing she had a concussion, which meant the longer she remained out of it, the more chance of complications.

"Ma'am? Sarah? Can you hear me?"

Her eyes blinked a little but remained closed, as if her subconscious didn't want to face the pain, either. He carefully ran his hands over her, avoiding the obvious arm fracture as he checked for other injuries. At least nothing else seemed obvious. With that basic information, he reached for his cell phone and quickly dialed 911.

He could drive her to the Pine Gulch medical clinic faster than the mostly volunteer fire department could gather at the station and come out to the ranch, but he was leery to move her without knowing if she might be suffering internal injuries.

As he gave the basic information to the dispatcher, her eyes started to flutter. An instant later, those eyes opened slightly, reminding him again of lazy summer afternoons when he was a kid and had time to gaze up at the sky. He saw confusion there and long, deep shadows of pain that filled him with guilt.

She had been cleaning his house. He couldn't help but feel responsible.

"Take it easy. You'll be okay."

She gazed at him for an instant with fright and uncertainty before he saw a tiny spark of recognition there.

"Mr....Bowman."

"Good. At least you know *my* name. How about your own?"

She blinked as if the effort to remember was too much. "S-Sarah. Sarah M—er, Whitmore."

He frowned at the way she stumbled a little over her last name but forgot it instantly when she shifted a little and tried to move. At the effort, she gave a heartbreaking cry of pain.

"Easy. Easy." He murmured the words as softly as he would to a skittish horse—if he were the sort of rancher to tolerate any skittish horses on the River Bow. "Just stay still."

"It hurts," she moaned.

"I know. I'm sorry. I'm afraid you broke your arm when you fell. I've called an ambulance. They should be here soon. We'll run you into the clinic in Pine Gulch. Dr. Dalton should be able to fix you up."

Her pale features grew even more distressed. "I don't need an ambulance," she said.

"I hate to argue with a lady, but I would have to disagree with you there. You took a nasty fall. Do you remember what happened?"

She looked up the stairs and her eyes widened. For a minute, he thought she would pass out again. "I was going to talk to you and I...I tripped, I guess. I'm not sure. Everything is fuzzy."

"You were coming to talk to me about what?"

A couple of high spots of color appeared on her cheeks. "I...can't remember," she said, and he was almost positive she was lying. On the other hand, he didn't know the woman; she had just suffered a terrible fall and was likely in shock.

She shifted again, moving her head experimentally, but then let it back down.

"My head hurts."

"I'm sure it does. I'm no expert, but I'm guessing you banged it up, too. You've probably got a concussion. Have you had one before?"

"Not...that I remember."

Did that mean she hadn't had one or that she just couldn't remember it? He would have to let Doc Dalton sort that one out from her medical records.

She started to moan but caught it, clamping her lips together before it could escape.

"Just hang on. Don't try to move. I wish I could give you a pillow or some padding or something. I know it's not comfortable there on the floor but you're better off staying put until the EMTs come and can assess the situation to make sure nothing else is broken. Can you tell me what hurts?"

"Everything," she bit out. "It's probably easier to tell you what *doesn't* hurt. I think my left eyelashes might be okay. No, wait. They hurt, too."

He smiled a little, admiring her courage and grit in the face of what must be considerable pain. He was also aware of more than a little relief. Though she grimaced between each word, he had to think that since she was capable of making a joke, she would probably be okay, all things considered.

"Is there somebody you'd like me to call to meet us at the hospital? Husband? Boyfriend? Family?"

She blinked at him, a distant expression on her face, and didn't answer him for a long moment.

"Stay with me," he ordered. Fearing she would lapse into shock, he grabbed a blanket off the sofa and spread it over her. For some reason, the shock first aid acronym of WARRR rang through his head: Warmth, Air, Rest, Reassurance, Raise the legs. But she seemed to collect herself enough to respond.

"No. I don't have…any of those things. There's no one in the area for you to call."

She was all alone? Somehow, he found that even more sad than the idea that she was currently sprawled out in grave pain on the floor at the bottom of his stairs.

His family might drive him crazy sometimes, but at least he knew they always had his back.

"Are you sure? No friends? No family? I should at least call the company you work for and let them know what happened."

If nothing else, they would have to send someone else to finish the job. With that broken arm, Sarah would have to hang up her broom for a while.

"I don't—" she started to say, but before she could finish, the front door opened and a second later an EMT raced through it, followed by a couple more.

Somehow he wasn't surprised that the EMT in the front was his brother Taft, who was not only a paramedic but also the town's fire chief.

He spotted the woman on the floor, and his forehead furrowed with confusion before he turned to Ridge.

"Geez. I just about had a freaking heart attack! We got a call for a female fall victim at the River Bow. I thought it was Destry!"

"No. This is Sarah Whitmore. She was cleaning the house after the wedding and took a tumble. Sarah, this is my brother Taft, who is not only a certified paramedic, I promise, but also the town's fire chief."

"Hi," she mumbled, sounding more disoriented

"Hi, Sarah." Taft knelt down to her and immediately went to work assessing vitals. "Can you tell me what happened?"

"I'm...not sure. I fell."

"Judging by the garbage at the top of the stairs, I think she fell just about the whole way," Ridge offered. "She was unconscious for maybe two or three minutes and has kind of been in and out since. My unofficial diagnosis is the obvious broken arm and possible concussion."

"Thank you, Dr. Bowman," Taft said, his voice dry.

His brother quickly took control of the situation and began giving instructions to the other emergency personnel.

Ridge was always a little taken by surprise whenever he had the chance to watch either of his younger brothers in action. He still tended to think of them as teenage punks getting speeding tickets and toilet papering the mayor's trees. But after years as a wildlands firefighter, Taft had been the well-regarded fire chief in Pine Gulch for several years, and his twin, Trace, was the police chief. By all reports, both were shockingly good at their jobs.

Ridge gained a little more respect for his brother as he watched his patient competence with Sarah: the way he teased and questioned her, the efficient air of command he portrayed to the other EMTs as they worked together to load her onto the stretcher with a minimum of pain.

As they started to roll the stretcher toward the front door, Ridge followed, grabbing his coat and truck keys on the way.

Taft shifted his attention away from his patient long enough to look at Ridge with surprise. "Where are you going?"

He was annoyed his brother would even have to ask. "I can't just send her off in an ambulance by herself. I'll drive in and meet you at the clinic."

"Why?" Taft asked, clearly confused.

"She doesn't have any friends or family in the area. Plus she was injured on the River Bow, which makes her my responsibility."

Taft shook his head but didn't argue. The stretcher

was nearly to the door when Sarah held out a hand. "Wait. Stop."

She craned her neck and seemed to be looking for him, so Ridge moved closer.

"You'll be okay." He did his best to soothe her. "Hang in there. My brother and the other EMTs will take good care of you, I promise, and Doc Dalton at the clinic is excellent. He'll know just what to do for you."

She barely seemed to register his words, her brow furrowed. Taft had given her something for pain before they transferred her, and it looked as if she was trying to work through the effects of it to tell him something.

"Can you… There's a case on the…backseat of my car. Can you bring it inside? I shouldn't have left it out in the cold…for this long. The keys to the car are…in my coat."

"Sure. No problem."

"You have to put it…somewhere safe." She closed her eyes as soon as the words were out.

Ridge raised an eyebrow at Taft, who shrugged. "It seems important to her," his brother said. "Better do it."

"Okay. I'll meet you at the clinic in a few minutes. I'll bring her coat along. Maybe I can find a purse or something in the car with her medical insurance information."

She hadn't been carrying anything like that when she came to the door, he remembered. Perhaps she found it easier to leave personal items in her vehicle.

He found her coat and located a single key in the pocket, hooked to one of the flexible plastic key rings with a rental car company's logo on it. He frowned. A rental car? That didn't make any sense. He headed outside to her vehicle, which was a nondescript silver sedan that did indeed look very much like a rental car.

He found a purse on the passenger seat, a flowered cloth bag. Though he was fiercely curious, he didn't feel right about digging through it. He would let her find her insurance info on her own.

In the backseat, he quickly found the case she was talking about. It was larger than he expected, a flat portfolio size, perhaps twenty-four inches by thirty or so.

Again, he was curious and wanted to snoop but forced himself not to. As she had requested, he set it in a locked cupboard in his office, then locked the office for good measure before heading to the clinic in town to be with a strange woman with columbine-blue eyes and the prettiest hair he'd ever seen.

As far as weird days went, this one probably just hit the top of the list.

Sarah hurt everywhere, but this was a muted sort of pain. She felt as if she were floating through a bowl of pudding. Nice, creamy, delicious chocolate pudding—except every once in a while something sharp and mean poked at her.

"All things considered, you got off easy. The concussion appears to be a mild one, and the break is clean." A man with a stethoscope smiled at her. No white coat, but white teeth. Handsome. He was really handsome. If she didn't hurt so much, she would tell him so.

"Easy?" she muttered, her mind catching on the word that didn't make sense.

The doctor smiled. "It could have been much worse, trust me. I've seen that staircase inside the River Bow. It has to be twenty feet, at least. It's amazing you didn't break more than your arm."

"Amazing," she agreed, though she didn't really know what he was talking about. What was the River Bow?

"And it's a good thing Ridge didn't move you right after you fell. I was able to set the arm without surgery, which I probably wouldn't have been able to do if you had been jostled around everywhere."

"Thank you," she said through dry lips, because it seemed to be the thing to say. She just wanted to sleep for three or four years. Why wouldn't he let her sleep?

"Can I go home?" she asked. Her condo, with its four-poster bed, the light blue duvet, the matching curtains. She wanted to be there.

"Where, exactly, is home?"

She gave the address to her condo unit.

"Is that in Idaho Falls?"

"No!" she exclaimed. "San Diego, of course."

He blinked a little. "Wow. You traveled a long way to take a cleaning job."

She frowned. Cleaning job? What cleaning job?

She wanted to rub away the fierce pain in her head even as she had a sudden image of a garbage bag with cups and napkins spilling out of it.

She had been cleaning something. Why? Is that when she fell? Her memories seemed hazy and abstract. She remembered an airplane. An important suitcase. *Hand-screen it, please.* An inn.

"I'm staying at the Cold Creek Inn," she said suddenly. Oh, she should have told them pain medication made her woozy. She always took only half. How much had they given her?

And how *had* she hurt her arm?

"The Cold Creek Inn." The nice doctor with the white teeth frowned at her.

"Yes. My room has blue curtains. They have flowers on them. They're pretty."

He blinked at her. "Good to know. Okay."

Oh, she was tired. Why wouldn't he let her sleep?

She closed her eyes but suddenly remembered something important. "Where's my car? Have you got my car? I have to take it back to the airport by Monday at noon or they'll charge me a *lot*."

"It must still be at the River Bow. I'm sure your car is fine."

"I have to take it back."

The car was important, but something else mattered more. Something in the car. But what?

Her head ached again, and one of those hard, ugly pains pierced that lovely haze.

"My head hurts," she informed him.

"That's your concussion. Just close your eyes and try to relax. We'll make sure the rental car goes back, I promise."

"Monday. Noon."

She needed something from inside it. She closed her eyes, seeing that special black suitcase again.

Oh.

Ridge Bowman. She had told Ridge Bowman to take it out of the backseat. Too cold. Not safe.

He would take care of it.

She wasn't sure how she knew, but a feeling of peace trickled over her, washing away the panic, and she let it go.

Chapter Three

"The Cold Creek Inn? Really?" Ridge stared at Jake Dalton, trying to make sense of a situation that seemed to be rapidly spinning out of his control.

"That's what she said. She was quite firm about it."

Pine Gulch's only physician had no reason to make up crazy stories but none of this was making any sense to him. "That's easy enough for me to verify. I can always give Laura a call."

Under normal circumstances, Taft's wife wouldn't disclose information about her guests, but this certainly classified as an emergency.

"Her car was a rental. I noticed that."

"Yes, it needs to be returned soon. She was quite emphatic on that score," Jake said.

"What the hell? She's staying at the Cold Creek Inn

and driving a rental car, and she shows up for a cleaning job? It doesn't make any sense."

"I'm only telling you what she said. That's not the important part, really. The fact is, if she indeed has no friends or family nearby, as she told you, I can't let our mystery woman go back to a hotel by herself tonight. She's suffered a concussion. She's going to need someone close by to make sure she doesn't suffer any complications. I can't say she really needs an overnight stay in the hospital in Idaho Falls, but I don't feel comfortable sending her back to a hotel to spend the night by herself."

While Ridge might've been baffled about the situation and why a woman paying for a decent hotel room and driving a rental car would take a low-paying cleaning job in the middle of nowhere, he wasn't at all confused about the right thing to do.

"She'll stay at the ranch house," he said firmly. "She can take Caidy's room, no problem. That way she won't have to tackle any stairs. Destry and I can keep an eye on her."

"Are you sure about that?" Jake asked in surprise. "You don't even know the woman."

True enough. All he knew was that she was lovely, that she smelled like vanilla and June-blooming lavender and that she brought out all his protective instincts.

He didn't think Jake Dalton needed those particular observations. "She was hurt in my house while technically working for me. That makes her my responsibility. If she had been hurt at the Cold Creek Ranch, you know any of you Daltons would jump up to take care of her. Wade and Seth would probably come to blows over who would help her, unless their wives stepped in first."

"You've got me there. The fact is, if my wife were

home, Ms. Whitmore could come stay at our place. But Maggie and her mother took an overnight trip to Jackson to do some Christmas shopping. I'm on my own with the kids and have my hands more than full."

The doctor grinned at him. "On second thought, sure you wouldn't like to trade? How about I come out to the quiet River Bow and keep an eye on our concussed woman of mystery and you can head over to my place and entertain three crazy kids hopped up on sugar and Christmas?"

He laughed. Jake and Maggie Dalton had three of the most adorable kids around, but they did have a lot of energy. "Well, that is a kind offer, I'm sure, but I would hate to deprive you of all that father–kid bonding time."

"Well, you've got my cell number. Call me if you have any concerns, particularly if you find any altered mental status or confusion." He paused and gave a little laugh. "I should probably warn you, though, she's a little, er, dopey from the pain meds. This doesn't count."

Jake's cautionary words made him more than a little curious. Sarah had seemed so contained back at his house. Even when her arm had to be screaming pain at her, she had fought tears and tried to be tough through it.

He walked into the treatment room, not quite sure what to expect.

Dopey was an understatement. Sarah Whitmore was higher than a weather balloon in a windstorm.

As soon as he walked into the room, she beamed at him like he had just rescued a basketful of kittens from a rampaging grizzly.

"Hi. Hi there. I know you, right?"

He glanced over at the doc, who just barely managed

to hide a grin. "Er, yes. I'm Ridge Bowman. You fell down my stairs a couple of hours ago."

"Oh. Riiiight." She beamed brightly at him. "Wow, you are one good-looking cowboy. Has anybody ever told you that?"

Jake made a sound halfway between a cough and a laugh. Ridge glared at him before he turned back to Sarah. "Er, not lately. No."

"Well, you are. Take it from me. Of course, what do I know? I don't know many good-looking cowboys. Or that many good-looking noncowboys, for that matter." She frowned, her features solemn. "I really need to get out more."

Jake laughed out loud, and Ridge gave him a quelling look. "Geez, how much did you give her?"

"Sorry," the physician said. "The dose was absolutely appropriate, but I'm thinking she must be one of those people who are hypersensitive to certain narcotics. Sometimes you have to titrate to an individual's particular sensitivities."

"Apparently. Okay, Sarah. Let's get you back to the ranch."

She started to stand up, but Jake laid a restraining hand on her shoulder. "Easy there. We'll bring in a wheelchair to get you out to the car."

"I can walk. I broke my arm, not my legs." She didn't precisely call Jake stupid, but her tone conveyed the same message.

"It's a clinic rule. Sorry, Sarah."

"Well, it's a dumb rule."

He chuckled. "I'll take it up with the clinic director when she gets back from shopping with her mother in

Jackson. Joan, can you bring a wheelchair?" he called out into the hall.

A moment later, one of the clinic nurses pushed in a chair. Jake and Ridge helped her transfer into it, with much grumbling on Sarah's part.

While Jake and the nurse pushed her toward the front of the clinic, Ridge went out to pull his truck up to the doors. Wishing he had brought the ranch SUV, which had a lower suspension and was easier to climb into, he tried to help her up into the cab. In the long run, he settled on lifting her up when she couldn't quite manage to navigate the running boards.

When she was settled, he shut the door to keep in all the heat and turned back to Jake.

"What else do I need to know?"

"You're going to want to make sure she drinks plenty of fluids tonight and keeps on a regular cycle of the pain meds, though you might want to dial that down a little. She'll probably sleep off most of what we gave her here. You'll want to check on her every couple of hours, make sure she's still lucid. Any problems, again, call my cell number. I should be home all night and can run to your place in a minute, though I might be dragging three kids along with me."

Ridge reached out to shake his hand, grateful for the other man. Jake Dalton had been good for Pine Gulch. He had the skills and the bedside manner that could probably have built a lucrative family medicine practice anywhere. Instead, he had chosen to come back to his own small hometown. In the years since, he and his wife, Magdalena Cruz, had really thrown their hearts into helping the community, sponsoring free clinics out of their own pockets and taking anybody who needed health care.

"I'm not worried. We should be fine."

"Are you sure? Maybe Becca or Laura can help," Jake suggested, referring to Ridge's sisters-in-law.

"I'll keep trying the cleaning company in Jackson. They might have an emergency contact number on her employment records."

"Good thinking. Drive safe. I think the storm is going to be here earlier than the weather forecasters said. No question about Pine Gulch having a white Christmas this year, I guess."

"Is there ever?" he said drily as he climbed into the pickup truck.

After making sure his guest was safely buckled in, he waved to Jake and backed out of the parking lot then headed toward the River Bow, a few miles out of town, through a lightly falling snow.

"Your truck smells like Christmas," she said, rather sleepily.

He pointed to the little air freshener shaped like an evergreen tree that hung from the rearview mirror. "You can give my daughter credit for that. She complains that it usually smells like shi—er, manure."

"You have a daughter?"

He nodded. "Yep. Destry's her name. She'll be twelve in a couple of months."

"Like the movie with James Stewart."

"Something like that." His late ex-wife had been fascinated with the old western *Destry Rides Again,* probably because she fancied herself a Marlene Dietrich wannabe. She had loved the name, and at that point, he would have done anything to try saving his marriage.

"Where is she?"

"Er, who?"

"Your daughter. Destry."

Ah. That was easy. Explaining that his ex-wife took off a few months after their daughter was born would have been tougher.

"She stayed at her cousin's house last night, but she's supposed to come home later tonight."

"Oh, that's nice. I have twenty-four kids."

He jerked his gaze from the road just long enough to gape at her. "Twenty-four?"

"Yes. Last year it was only twenty-two. The year before that, I had twenty-five. I had the biggest class in the first grade."

"You're a teacher?"

She nodded, though her head barely moved on the headrest and her eyes began to drift closed. "Yes," she mumbled. "I teach first grade at Sunny View Elementary School. I'm a great teacher."

"I'm sure you are. But I thought you worked for the cleaning service."

She frowned a little, opening her eyes in confusion before they slid shut again. "I'm soooo tired. My head hurts."

Just like that, she was asleep.

"Sarah? Ms. Whitmore?"

She snorted and shifted in her sleep. The mystery deepened. The woman was staying at the inn, drove a rental car and apparently taught first grade.

He knew teachers weren't paid nearly enough. Maybe she had picked up extra work during the school break, but that didn't explain the inn or the rental car.

His cell phone rang just as he pulled into the long,

winding lane that led from the main road to the ranch house. "Ridge Bowman," he answered.

"Oh, Mr. Bowman," the flustered voice on the other end of the line exclaimed. "This is Terri McCall from Happy House Cleaners in Jackson. There's been a terrible mix-up. I'm so sorry! You would not *believe* the day we've had here."

He glanced at the woman sleeping on the bench seat beside him. "Mine hasn't been exactly a walk in the park, either."

"It's been chaos from the moment I walked in this morning. Our power was knocked out in the night and we're only just getting back up. Meantime, all the computers were down. I just saw your name on my caller ID and realized we had your dates wrong, so I've been scrambling to find someone else. I had you down for party cleanup tomorrow. I'm *so* sorry. I'm sending someone right now. She should be there within the hour, I promise, and we'll have you sorted out."

He gazed at the woman sleeping beside him. "Wait a minute. What about Sarah?"

He was met with a little awkward pause. "The woman I'm sending is Kelli Parker. She'll do a fine job. I'm afraid I don't know a Sarah."

"Sarah. Sarah Whitmore. I left you a message about her. We're just coming from the doctor. She broke her arm and had a concussion in the fall."

"Oh, I'm sorry. I haven't had time to listen to my messages, with everything that's been going on. Do you need us to clean her house, too?"

"No. She works for you! She showed up this morning to clean for me. In the process, she tripped and fell down my stairs."

"This is all very strange." The woman sounded baffled and a little concerned. "We don't have anyone named Sarah working for us and, as I said, we had the dates switched."

"You didn't send someone."

"Yes. Just now," she said patiently. "Not earlier this morning. Kelli Parker. She's very efficient. One of our very best, I promise you."

"So if you didn't send someone to clean my house, who the hell is this woman sitting next to me with the broken arm and the concussion?"

"I'm sure I don't know. She's not my employee, I can promise you that. Why would anybody want to pretend to be? Perhaps you had better call the police."

He pulled up in front of the ranch house and sat in the truck for a moment, the phone still pressed to his ear. He didn't want to call the police. In Pine Gulch, the police meant his brother Trace. Bad enough that Taft had to come out on the emergency call and find a strange woman crumpled at the bottom of the stairs. Trace would never let him hear the end of this one.

"Okay. Thank you. I'll watch for your actual employee."

"I'm sorry again for the mix-up. I don't want you to think we usually conduct our business in this scatterbrained way. The holidays have been crazy anyway, with everybody wanting sparkling houses for their parties and overnight guests, and six hours without electricity or computers didn't help matters."

"No problem. Thanks."

He hung up and looked across the cab at Sarah. A strand of auburn hair had drifted across her cheek, accentuating the complexion that was still too pale for his liking.

He would sure like to figure out just what the hell was going on, but he wasn't quite ready to call the police. Trace had an annoying tendency to take over in matters of an investigative nature, and Ridge was feeling oddly territorial about this woman.

He figured he could get her settled and then if she was still out of it, he could go through her purse and try to find out why a woman who claimed she taught first grade at Sunny View Elementary School decided to spend a little time cleaning up the party mess at a ranch house in some small backwater Idaho town.

She didn't appear to wake even after he shut off the engine and walked around to the passenger door. "Here we are. Let's get you inside. Can you walk, or do I have to carry you?"

She opened her eyes for just a moment before closing them again. That was apparently all the answer he was going to get. He sighed and scooped her into his arms, thinking again how slight and delicate she was. She hardly weighed more than Destry.

She was definitely a curvy little handful, though. He tried not to notice, tried to remind himself she was a mysterious stranger who had entered his home under false pretenses, tried not to remember how very long it had been since he'd held a sweet-smelling woman in his arms.

He carried her up the stairs to the mudroom and then through the kitchen to the hallway that led to Caidy's downstairs bedroom.

In contrast to everything else about his hard-riding, horse-training, dog-loving sister, her bedroom was soft and feminine, with a lavender and brown quilt joining a flurry of pillows on the bed and lace curtains spilling from the window.

The room might have been made for Sarah. She had a kind of sweet, ethereal beauty that fit perfectly with all of Caidy's frills.

She moaned a little when he lowered her to the bed and he quickly propped one of Caidy's hundreds of throw pillows underneath her casted arm.

"There. Is that better?"

Her eyes fluttered open, and she looked around, still with that vaguely unfocused look.

"This isn't my hotel room," she said, her voice a husky rasp.

"No. You're temporarily staying at the River Bow ranch."

"I need to talk to the Bowman family," she stated, still dreamily. "It's really important."

This whole thing was so strange. What was she doing here? What did she need to talk to his family about? He frowned as he eased away from her, but she had already closed her eyes again.

She didn't look at all comfortable. After a pause, he reached down and slipped off her shoes, but that was about as far as he dared go.

He grabbed a soft fleece blanket from the foot of the bed and tucked it under her chin, then stood back and studied her.

What an odd day. Why couldn't he shake the strange feeling that something momentous was happening? He didn't like it, especially because he didn't understand it.

After a moment, he gave her one more careful look then turned and walked from the bedroom. The sun went down early on a late-December afternoon. In another hour, it would be dark, which meant he needed to hustle out to take care of chores. He was a rancher, which meant he didn't have all day to stand and look at his mysterious guest, no matter how lovely she might be.

Chapter Four

Sarah awoke to a mouth as dry as the Mojave in August and, conversely, a desperate need to use the bathroom.

She opened her eyes slowly and tried to make sense of where she was, why the room didn't look familiar. A lamp glowed beside the bed, illuminating a comfortably feminine room. A plump armchair stood in one corner and just next to it, she could see an open doorway that looked like it contained the facilities she needed.

When she sat up, a grinding wave of pain washed over her. Her head and her left arm seemed to be the focus of most of the pain but the rest of her body felt as if she had just ridden out the permanent press cycle on a front-loading washing machine.

By the time she hobbled back out of the nicely decorated en suite bathroom, vague, rather unsettling memories were beginning to filter through.

She was at the Bowman family's River Bow ranch—
she could tell by the log walls and the general decor of
the place. She had fallen down the stairs while she was
cleaning the ranch house after Caidy Bowman's wedding.

She remembered Ridge Bowman, suddenly—piercing
green eyes, hard features, broad shoulders. He thought
she was from a cleaning company, and she had been too
much of a coward to tell him otherwise.

She remembered an ambulance ride with a man who
had Ridge Bowman's same handsome features and those
stunning green eyes.

The actual trip from the clinic to the ranch house was
mostly a blur of random impressions, pain and confusion and embarrassment. There had been a kind doctor,
a painful procedure and then the rest was a blur.

Why was she back at the River Bow and not at her
room at the Cold Creek Inn? And how had she ended
up in that bed with her shoes off and a pillow tucked
under her arm?

It must have been Ridge. Who else? Her stomach
trembled when she thought about him taking care of
her. Had he carried her inside? Slipped her onto the bed?
Covered her with that blanket?

She could hardly imagine it.

She had to talk to him, right away, before things became even more complicated. She wouldn't be in this
mess if only she had been able to find the courage to tell
him everything when she showed up on his doorstep,
instead of letting her fear at what he might think of her
overwhelm all her good sense.

How long had she slept? She couldn't see anything
outside the fragile lace curtains. She found the clock

radio beside the bed and was shocked to discover it was after 9:00 p.m. She must have been out of it for hours, though she wasn't exactly sure how long she had been at the clinic in Pine Gulch.

She was just trying to gather the energy and the courage to go in search of her unwilling host when she heard a knock on the door.

"Ms. Whitmore? Are you awake?"

Nerves trembled through her to join the aches and pains. "Yes. Come in."

He pushed open the door and stood there wearing a soft-looking blue shirt and jeans.

You are one great-looking cowboy.

The words seemed to echo through her memory, and she frowned, wondering where they came from. Not that it mattered—they were absolutely true. Ridge Bowman was even more handsome than she remembered, tough and rugged, with shoulders that looked as if they could bear the weight of the world.

"I'm under orders from Doc Dalton to keep an eye on you through the night. I guess I'm supposed to make sure you're not delusional or anything."

She thought of the crazy choices she had made since she showed up at the ranch that morning. Really. Cleaning the man's house as an avoidance method. Could she *be* any more ridiculous?

"I was half hoping this whole thing was some kind of wild nightmare," she said. "Does that count as delusional?"

The corner of his mouth danced up just a bit as if he wanted to smile, but he quickly straightened it again. "I'm supposed to check. Do you know your name?"

"Yes. Sarah Whitmore."

"That's what your driver's license says."

He was holding out her bag, which looked incongruously feminine in his big, masculine hand.

"You looked through my purse?"

"I was trying to find a cell phone that had an emergency contact on it. I couldn't find one."

She didn't go *anywhere* without her cell phone. She frowned, trying to remember. "Did you check the car? It might be there. Otherwise, I probably left it at the hotel."

"I'll look through the car again. Maybe it fell on the floor. I can also have Laura look at the hotel."

"Why don't you just take me back to the hotel and I can look for myself?"

He looked sternly implacable. "You can't stay on your own tonight. Doctor's orders. And as great as the service is now at the Cold Creek Inn since Laura took over, she just can't send a desk clerk to your room every couple of hours to check on you. I'm afraid you're stuck here, at least overnight."

She wanted to argue, but she couldn't come up with the words, between the pain and her angst.

Some of her distress must have shown on her features. He held out a water glass she hadn't noticed before, along with a bottle of medication.

"You're also late for your pain pill. Sorry about that. I was supposed to give it an hour ago, but I had a problem down at the barn and now I'm running late."

She didn't want to take it—she and pain medication didn't always get along—but she could hardly think around the pain in her head and her arm.

"Maybe I had better only take half. I sometimes get a little, er, wacky on pain meds."

"Do you?"

Again, that little corner of his mouth twisted up, and she had to wonder what had happened during the time she couldn't remember.

He broke the pill in half and held it out to her. She swallowed it quickly, more grateful for the water than the narcotic, at least right at that moment.

She drained the glass then handed it back to him. "Thank you."

"Need something to eat? I've got plenty of leftover food from the wedding last night and you haven't had a thing for hours."

"I'm not really hungry," she said honestly.

"I'll bring you a couple of things anyway. That pain medication will sit better in your stomach if you've got something else in there."

He was gone for only a few moments. When he returned, he had a plate loaded with little sandwiches, puff pastries, tiny bite-sized pieces of cake. He was also accompanied by the cute little Chihuahua who hopped in on three legs.

"Your dog is adorable."

"Destry and I are supposed to be dogsitting, but she stayed another night at her cousin's. This is Tripod, who belongs to my new brother-in-law and his kids."

"Hi, Tripod," she said to the dog, who hopped over to greet her with gratifying enthusiasm, though he might have been more interested in the plate of food on her lap.

She took a little sandwich and nibbled on it, discovering some kind of chicken salad that was quite delicious.

"These are really good."

"We had a great caterer," he said.

She suddenly remembered what had started all this. "Oh. I didn't finish cleaning."

He gave her a long look. "Happy House Cleaners and I have worked all that out. Their real employee just left about an hour ago. I'm surprised you didn't hear her vacuuming. I guess you were really out of it."

Apparently she didn't need to tell him as much as she thought, if he knew she hadn't really been hired to help clean his house.

"I've made a terrible mess of everything, haven't I?"

"You're a woman of mystery, that's for sure. Who are you, really, Ms. Whitmore?"

She nibbled at another of the little sandwiches. "You looked through my purse. You tell me."

He gave her a long look, filled with curiosity and something else—something almost like male interest, though she knew she had to be mistaken. From a quick look in the bathroom mirror while she washed her hands, she knew she was a mess. Her hair was flattened on one side where she had been sleeping, she had a couple of really ugly bruises and her eyes looked inordinately huge in her face. Like she was some kind of creepy bug or something.

"Didn't tell me much, if you want the truth," he answered. "You like cinnamon Altoids. You live in Apartment 311 of the Cyprus Grove complex in San Diego. You have a school district ID card, and your birthday is March 14, when you'll be twenty-nine years old. Funny, but I couldn't find a single thing in your purse that might explain why you showed up at my ranch out of the blue and started cleaning up for me."

She could feel her face heat with her ready blush, the redhead's curse. "You assumed that's why I was here. I tried to tell you otherwise but you seemed in a rush to go back to your office. Besides, I could tell you really did need help."

"I absolutely did, which is why I hired someone who wasn't you to take care of it," he pointed out. "Since you weren't here to clean, why *did* you show up on my doorstep?"

She chewed her lip, trying to figure out the best way to explain.

"Oh! I have a case in my rental car," she exclaimed suddenly, horrified at her negligence. "I need to bring it in from the cold. Oh, I can't believe I forgot it!"

"Relax. You didn't forget. It's locked in my office right now. Don't you remember telling me to bring it inside just as Taft and the other paramedics were carrying you out to the ambulance?"

She had a vague memory that seemed to drift in and out of her mind like a playful guppy.

She exhaled with relief. "Oh, good."

"So is the mysterious case the reason you're here?"

She sighed, knowing she couldn't avoid this any longer. "Could you get it?"

He eased away from the door frame, his expression wary. After a moment, he left the room. As she waited for him to return, she closed her eyes, dreading the next few moments.

The past five days had been such a blur. From the moment she found the receipt for a storage unit while clearing out her father's papers, she felt as if she had been on a crazy roller coaster, spinning her in all directions.

After seeing the contents of that storage unit, she had a hundred vague, horrible suspicions but they were all surreal, insubstantial. None of it seemed real—probably because she didn't *want* it to be real.

Her research online had unearthed a chilling story, one she still couldn't quite comprehend, and one she didn't want to believe had anything to do with her or any member of her family.

She had packed up one piece of evidence and brought it here in hopes of finding out the truth. Now that she was here, she realized how foolish her hopes had been. What was she expecting? That she would find out everything had just been a horrible mistake?

She waited, nerves stretched taut. When he returned, the black portfolio looked dark and forbidding in his arms.

"Here you go." He handed it to her, and she moved to the bed.

"Did you look inside, like you looked in my purse?"

He shook his head. "I didn't want to invade your privacy, but circumstances didn't leave me much choice."

She was glad for that, at least. With her only workable hand, she opened the case and slid out the contents, resting it on the blanket.

The loveliness still caught her breath—a beautiful painting of a pale lavender columbine so real she could almost smell it, cupped in both hands of a small blonde girl who looked to be about three years old.

Ridge Bowman's expression seemed to freeze the moment he caught sight of the painting. His jaw looked hard as granite.

"Where did you get that?" he demanded, his voice harsh.

Instinctively, she wanted to shrink from that tone. She hated conflict and had since she was a little girl listening to her parents scream at each other.

She swallowed hard. "My…father recently died, and I found it among his things."

He wasn't angry, she suddenly realized. He was overwhelmed.

"It's even more beautiful than I remember," he said, his tone almost reverent. He traced a finger over the edge of one petal, and she realized with shock that this big, tough rancher looked as if he was about to weep.

Who was this man who looked as if he could wrestle a steer without working up a sweat but who could cry over a painting of a little girl holding a flower?

"It…belonged to your family, then?"

He looked up as if he had forgotten she was there. "This is why you came to the ranch?"

She nodded, a movement that reminded her quite forcibly of her aching head. "When I found it," she said carefully, "I immediately did a web search for the artist. Margaret Bowman."

"My mother."

He looked at the painting again, his expression more soft than she had seen it.

As she watched him, Sarah was suddenly overwhelmed with exhaustion, so very tired of carrying the weight of her past and trying to stay ahead of demons she could never escape.

She shouldn't have come here. It had been foolishly impulsive and right now she couldn't believe she ever thought it might be a good idea to face the Bowman family in person.

If she had been thinking straight, she simply would have tracked down an email address and sent a photograph of the painting with her questions. Better yet, she should have had her attorney contact the Bowman family.

Her only explanation for the choices that had led her here had been her own reaction to the paintings. She had been struck by all of them, particularly this one—by its artistic merit and the undeniable skill required to make simple pigment leap from the canvas like that, but also by the obvious love the artist had for the child in the painting.

"Do you have any idea where your father obtained this painting?" Ridge asked her.

Suspicions? Yes. Proof, on the other hand, was something else entirely. She shook her head, which wasn't a lie.

"It means a great deal to you, doesn't it?" she said carefully.

"If you only knew. I thought we would never see it again. Of everything, this is the one I missed most of all. That's my sister, Caidy, in the painting. The one whose wedding we had here yesterday."

She had suspected as much. Somehow that made everything seem more heartbreaking. "She was a lovely child," she said softly.

"Who grew into an even lovelier woman." He smiled, and she was suddenly aware of a fierce envy at the relationship between Ridge Bowman and his family members. The family was obviously very close, despite the tragedy that must have affected all of them.

She thought of her half brother and their tangled relationship. She had loved him dearly when she was young, despite the decade age difference between them. In the end, he had become a stranger to her.

"How much do you want for it?" Ridge asked abruptly. "Name your price."

"What?" she exclaimed.

"That's why you came, isn't it?" He raised an eyebrow, and she didn't mistake the shadow of derision in his eyes that hadn't been there before.

He thought she was trying to extort money from the family, she realized with horror. She was so startled, she didn't answer for several seconds.

He must have taken her silence for a negotiation tactic. His mouth tightened and he frowned. "I should be coy here, pretend I don't really want it, maybe try to bargain with you a little. I don't care. I want it. Name your price. If it's at all within reason, I'll pay it."

She shook her head. "I—I don't want your money, Mr. Bowman."

"Don't you?"

"When I read the stories online about your parents and their…" Her voice trailed off, and she didn't quite know how to finish that statement.

"Their murders?"

She shivered a little at his bluntness. "Yes," she said. "Their murders. When I read the news reports and realized the artist of that beautiful painting had died, I knew I had to come. The painting is yours. I won't let you pay me anything. I fully intended to give it back to you and your family."

"You what?" He clearly didn't believe her.

"I have no legal or moral claim to it. It rightfully belongs to your family. It's yours."

He stared at her and then back at the painting, brow furrowed. "What's the catch?"

"No catch. It's yours," she repeated.

She didn't add the rest. Not yet. She would have to tell him, but he was so shocked about her volunteering this painting to him, she wasn't quite ready to let him know everything else.

"I can't believe this. You have no idea. It's like having a piece of her back. My mother, I mean."

The love in his voice touched a chord somewhere deep inside. She thought of her own mother, bitter and angry at the world and the cards she had been dealt. Her mother had raised her alone from the time Sarah was very young, working two jobs to support them because she wouldn't take money from her ex-husband. Sarah had loved her but accepted now that her mother had never been a kind woman. Barbara didn't have a lot of room left over around her hatred of Sarah's father to find love for the daughter they had created together.

"Can you tell me," she asked him, "was this piece part of the…stolen collection?"

After a moment, he nodded, his features dark.

What other answer had she expected? Sarah pressed her lips together. She couldn't tell him the rest. The dozens of pieces of art she had found in that climate-controlled storage unit.

She also couldn't tell him what she suspected.

She was suddenly exhausted, so tired her eyes felt gritty and heavy. She wanted nothing but to sleep again, to ease the pain of her injuries and the worse pain in her heart.

"Do you have any idea how your father obtained it?" he asked. "We've only found two or three pieces from the stolen collection in all these years. They seem to appear out of thin air, and we can never trace them back to the original seller. This could be just what we need to solve the case."

She couldn't tell him that. She didn't have the strength or the courage right now when she was hurting so badly. She would have her father's estate attorney deal with all the particulars, as she should have done from the beginning.

He would eventually know everything, but she wouldn't have to face those piercing green eyes during the telling.

"I've told you all I can. I found it among my father's things, as I said, and now I would like you and your family to have it. Take the painting, Mr. Bowman. Ridge. Please. Consider it a Christmas gift if you want, but it's yours."

"I can't believe this. I'm…stunned." He smiled at her, a flash of bright joy that took her breath away. "Thank you. Thank you so much. I can't begin to tell you how happy Caidy, Taft and Trace will be. You've given us a gift beyond price."

"I'm glad." She mustered a smile, even though it made her cheeks ache. "I'm so tired. Can I rest now?"

"Yes. Of course." He picked up the painting from the bed and held it gingerly, as if he couldn't quite believe it was in his hands again. "Caidy left a lot of her clothes here. Would you like me to find a nightgown for you to change into so you can be more comfortable?"

"I can do that. Thank you."

"You have nothing to thank me for. Not after this." He gestured to the painting in his hands. "I'm supposed to check on you a couple more times in the night. I'll apologize in advance for waking you."

"Apology accepted."

He headed for the door. "If you need anything else, call out. I'll probably sleep on the sofa in the family room off the kitchen."

She wanted to tell him that wasn't necessary, that she would be fine, but she was just too exhausted to argue—especially when she somehow knew he wouldn't listen anyway.

Chapter Five

Ridge closed the door behind him with one hand, the other still holding the miraculously returned painting. He stood in the hallway for a long moment and just gazed down at it, wondering what on earth had just happened in there.

He felt odd, off balance, not sure what to think or feel.

Something major had just happened. It wasn't only that she had returned this painting he thought he would never see again. He had felt a link between them, a tensile connection that seemed to seethe and pulse between them.

Or maybe that had been a figment of his imagination. Maybe it was simply late and he was tired after a long, strange day.

He carried the painting to his office and propped it

on a chair across from his desk where he could look at it and remember.

The painting was created with tenderness, out of a mother's love. That came through in every single brushstroke. Caidy would be so pleased to have it back in the family. She should really be the one to have it. Though he supposed it wasn't technically his to give, as it belonged to all of them as joint heirs to their parents' estate, maybe he could talk to Taft and Trace about the three of them giving it to their sister as a wedding present.

He looked at that sweet little girl in the painting cupping a fragile flower and her whole future in her hands and couldn't help but think of his own sweet little girl. Destry had grown up without a mother's love—though not really, when he thought about it. Caidy had stepped up to play that role after Melinda left, and had done an admirable job.

He frowned, wondering why his thoughts seemed to be so focused on his ex-wife today. He hadn't thought about her this much in months, not since early spring when he had finally paid a private detective to track her down, for Destry's sake.

As he had half suspected all these years, the trail was cold. The private detective had discovered Melinda had died just a year after she left them, killed along with her then-boyfriend in a car accident in Italy, of all places.

He hadn't grieved, only brooded for a few days about his own foolish choices and for a wild young woman who had never wanted to be a mother.

Any grief for his failed marriage had worked its way out of his system a long time ago, as he had rocked his crying child to sleep or put her on the bus by himself on the first day of school.

He suddenly missed his daughter fiercely. The house seemed entirely too quiet without her constant activity—either watching something on TV or chattering with Caidy.

On impulse, he dialed Trace's number. His brother answered the phone on the second ring.

"Missing Destry already?" his brother teased.

"Already?" He stretched back in his chair, suddenly tired from the tumultuous day. "It's been almost twenty-four hours. I missed her as soon as you drove away last night. Aren't you like that with Gabi and Will?"

His wife Becca had given birth over the summer to the most adorable little boy, all big blue eyes and lots of dark hair. Gabrielle wasn't Trace's daughter, she was actually Becca's much-younger sister, but the two of them had legal custody of her and loved her as their own child.

"I guess you're right. I was a mess in the fall when she went away for that school trip to the Teton Science School and that was only four nights."

"Are the girls having a good time?" he asked.

"I don't know. I've been working. I do know everybody's been sneaking around doing Christmassy things all day."

Now that the business of the wedding was over, he supposed he should probably start thinking about Christmas, only three days away.

He wasn't crazy about the holidays. None of the Bowman siblings were, considering their parents had been killed just a few days before Christmas.

Or at least none of them *used* to enjoy the season. It seemed as each of his siblings found love and moved on with life, each had been able to let go of those ghosts and embrace the holidays again. Caidy had even chosen this weekend for her wedding, claiming she wanted to be able to celebrate the season and not continue to mourn.

He gazed across the desk at the sweet little girl in the picture as his brother spoke.

"I hear you had some excitement on the ranch today."

"Did you?"

"I caught the ambulance call on the scanner, and Taft filled me in on the details. What are you doing, trying to kill the hired help?"

He didn't want to go into the whole story, but he suddenly realized he had called his brother's house not just to speak with his daughter but also for Trace's perspective on the situation.

"Sarah isn't the hired help," he explained. "Turns out, we had a little case of mistaken identity. When she showed up this morning, I made a leap and just assumed she was from the cleaning service. Turns out, she wasn't. When she saw what a mess the house was in after the wedding, she pitched in anyway to help me out and that's how she was injured."

"Wait a minute. She wasn't even from the cleaning company?"

Trace sounded both skeptical and suspicious. Justifiably so, he supposed.

"No. They had a mix-up in dates, but it's all been taken care of now. They sent somebody else this afternoon."

"So who is the injured lady and why was she there?"

"That is kind of a long story," he began, not quite sure how to explain what sounded implausible even to him.

"Yeah?"

"It's the craziest damn thing." He shifted in his seat. "She brought us one of the paintings."

A long pause met his words. "Which one?" Trace finally asked.

"One of Mom's. The one she did of Caidy up on the Pine Bend trail, with the columbine."

Trace was again silent. When he spoke, his voice was soft, with the same sort of reverence Ridge felt about it.

"I always loved that one," he said.

"Same here. It's even better than I remembered. She had amazing talent. It's no wonder her paintings sell for so much now."

The few paintings in circulation—those she had sold or given to friends before her death—were beginning to fetch in the high five figures, something that would have astonished their mother.

They had been able to track down a few pieces from the collection and had purchased what they could over the years but the few available were becoming as valued as they were rare.

"So let me get this straight," Trace said, his voice hard. "A woman just shows up out of the blue, almost exactly on the anniversary of the murders, with one of the paintings…and then supposedly injures herself while pretending to be something she isn't?"

He instinctively wanted to defend Sarah against the suspicions, even though he understood it and knew just where it originated. He couldn't blame his brother for questioning the situation.

Becca and Gabi's estranged mother, Monica, was an amoral con artist who had played a part, albeit a small one, in the planned robbery of the Bowmans' extensive art collection twelve years earlier.

Trace had a right to be mistrustful—though in Sarah's case, Ridge was quite certain it was unfounded.

"She broke her arm, Trace. Jake Dalton x-rayed it. If she's running a con, she certainly ramped things up a level or twelve by purposely fracturing her own arm."

He decided not to mention to his brother that too much pain medication made her act like a woozy sorority girl during pledge week. Any savvy con artist likely knew that about herself and would have taken pains to avoid it.

"I'm just saying the whole thing seems a little odd," Trace said. "Where did she say she obtained the painting?"

"Her father recently died and she found it among his things."

"Convenient."

He frowned, becoming annoyed now at his brother's tone. "Say what you want, but she came to the River Bow to return the painting to the family. She says it rightfully belongs to us, and she can't in good conscience keep it. She came all the way from California to give it back to us."

Even as he heard the words, he sensed how incredible they sounded. A little doubt began to creep in. Was she keeping something else from them? No. He didn't believe it. She was lovely and sweet, and he hadn't had nearly enough lovely, sweet things in his life lately.

"Where is she staying?" Trace asked. "At the inn?"

He again shifted in his chair. He wasn't about to lie to his brother, though he seriously disliked feeling like he was being interrogated here.

"She's here. In Caidy's room. Not only did she break her arm falling down the stairs but she also suffered a concussion. Doc Dalton didn't want her to stay by herself at the inn."

Trace didn't say anything, but Ridge could still feel the disapproval radiating from him.

"Be careful," his brother said. "That's all. Just be careful."

"Thanks for the advice, Mom. You mind if I talk to my daughter now?"

"I'll get her."

He drummed his fingers while he waited for Destry to come on the line.

"Hey, Dad! I heard you had some excitement there today. Trace told Aunt Becca you had to call the ambulance. I'm super glad you weren't the one who broke your arm! That would have been hard at Christmas."

One of his life's greatest joys was the knowledge that his daughter was growing to be a compassionate human being, who cared more about others than herself. Three Christmases ago, she had wanted to give all the money her family would have spent on her Christmas gifts to Gabi. He grinned at the sudden memory. At the time, Gabi had been a confused and scared young girl, abandoned by a ruthless mother. She had been trying to find her way in the world and had convinced Destry and all her little friends that she was dying and her family couldn't afford the surgery that would save her life.

Gabi had come such a long way now that she lived in a safe, comfortable home where she never doubted she was safe. She had become a healthy, well-adjusted young woman, and he loved her as if she were indeed his niece.

"So the cleaning lady was pretty hurt, huh?" Destry asked now.

He sighed. Apparently he would have to give the report to everybody in the family. It would have been easier to get them all on a blasted conference call. "She's doing all right. She's staying here for tonight, in Caidy's room. It's a long story."

"Okay," Destry said. Her easy acceptance made him smile.

"You really want to stay another night? I can run in and get you, no problem."

"We're in the middle of making a couple of Christmas projects—don't ask me what because I won't tell you. They won't be done until tomorrow. If you really need me, I guess Gabi can finish up on her own."

"No. It's fine. The house is just quiet with both you and Caidy gone."

"I'll be back tomorrow."

"Well, have a great time. Don't keep your aunt and uncle up all night with your giggling."

"Who us? Gabi and I don't giggle."

Ridge could just picture her batting her eyes innocently. He harrumphed. "Yeah, like I don't snore."

She laughed. "You're a nut. Good thing I love you, isn't it?"

"Good thing. I love you, too, ladybug. I'll see you tomorrow."

He hung up, missing her all over again. Though his marriage had been a mistake from the beginning, he would do it all over again in order to have Destry for a daughter.

Melinda had never been cut out for marriage to a rancher—neither the marriage part nor the living-on-a-ranch part.

His parents had seen it from the beginning and had tried to warn him, but he wouldn't listen, too enamored of this vibrant, beautiful woman who claimed to adore him.

He met her while he had taken a temporary job in Montana consulting with a movie star trying to start a hobby ranch. Melinda had been the personal assistant to the movie star's wife. She had been fascinated by cowboys and the West, and to his shocked delight, this wild, beautiful creature had somehow been fascinated with *him*.

For a month or so they had what he thought of as a fling, fiery and exciting. All that heat had already started to burn itself out when she came to him one night and told him she was pregnant. She had treated it with a casualness that had shocked him—"Oh, by the way, I missed my period. The pregnancy test was positive. Isn't that funny?"—as if the world hadn't just been shaken on its axis at the reality that the two of them had created life together.

He snorted now, remembering how he had automatically assumed they would marry. The way he was raised, that was just what a man did: he stepped up to take care of his responsibilities.

She had laughed at him and treated him like the provincial cowboy he was, but eventually he had persuaded her they could build a life together, for the sake of their child.

His parents hadn't approved of her or their marriage.

He eyed that painting again. The memory still burned. At the time of their deaths, the relationship between them had been strained and distant. Just the night before their murders, he had yelled at his father on the phone when Frank suggested maybe they hadn't known each other long enough for such a big step.

It was a hell of a thing that he let things become so tense between them without trying to heal the rift. He hated knowing his father died with Ridge's ugly words still ringing in his ears.

The worst part was, they were absolutely right about her. She *wasn't* cut out for this life, and both of them knew it. After his parents' deaths, he had no choice but to return to the River Bow to take over the ranch. Neither Taft nor Trace was in a position to do it, even if they'd wanted to.

He wanted to think Melinda had done her best, but a year after they moved to Pine Gulch and the River Bow, she had grown tired of being both a mother and a wife. Or at least being *his* wife. She had left both him and Destry one night with a hastily scribbled note that she was sorry but she couldn't do it anymore. She signed over full custody of Des, sent him divorce papers a few weeks later and disappeared.

For six months or so, she would send him emails from this spot or that one and then the correspondence became increasingly infrequent before it ended abruptly. He had suspected something had happened to her, but none of her friends could even tell him where she was when they heard from her last, and he didn't know how to start looking.

He really should have tried harder to find out, for Destry's sake if not his own, but he really wasn't sure he wanted to know the truth.

His thoughts turned to his unwilling houseguest. She was from California, too. She was also beautiful and soft. He wanted to think that was the extent of the similarities between her and Melinda—but he had learned his lesson well.

His ranch and his family. That's all he had time for, and he intended to keep things that way.

He certainly didn't have room for lovely injured schoolteachers with big blue eyes and secrets they didn't seem inclined to share.

Sarah woke from painkiller-twisted dreams to find a man standing in her doorway, big and hulking in the darkness. For an instant, icy panic swamped her, and her mind froze with nightmare fears of intruders and menacing strangers. A tiny, frightened sound escaped before she could swallow it back.

"Easy. Easy, Sarah. It's only me. Ridge Bowman."

The low, familiar voice acted on her like a comforting cup of chamomile tea. "Oh. Hi."

"Sorry I scared you. I warned you that Doc Dalton wanted me to check on you in the night. That's all I'm doing."

She drew in a calming breath and then another and willed the last shadow of panic to subside. "Of course. I remember."

"Mind if I turn on a lamp?"

"No. Go ahead."

A moment later, he flipped a switch and a small, comforting circle of light from a lamp on one of the bureaus pushed more of her panic away.

"There. Is that better?"

"Much. Sorry, I just woke up disoriented and forgot where I was for a moment."

He moved into the room. "Understandable. You've had quite a day. Anyone would be a little discombobulated, a word my mother used to love."

His mother, who had been murdered. She shivered and drew the quilts up higher as he moved closer to the bed.

"I'm supposed to make sure your brain is still working. Can you tell me what day it is?"

She closed her eyes and tried to think. Her arm and head both still ached, she realized, but without the insistent sharpness of before.

"Um, Saturday, right? Three days before Christmas."

"Technically it's Sunday now, but you're on the right track."

She glanced at the clock by the bed and saw it was after midnight.

"And what's your name again?"

"Sarah Whitmore," she answered promptly.

"What's my name?"

"You just reminded me two minutes ago. Ridge Bowman. Not that I would have forgotten. It's kind of an unusual name."

"That it is."

"Can I ask how you came by it?"

He leaned a hip against the footboard of the bed and she was suddenly keenly aware of him, his solid strength and leashed muscles.

"My parents met in Colorado while both of them were going to school there," he said, a small smile softening the hard lines and angles of his features. "Apparently one day Mom went hiking with her painting gear and ended up taking a bit of a tumble off a steep trail—she didn't fall far and wasn't hurt, but she was stranded on an isolated ledge for a couple of hours."

"Oh, no!"

"My father happened to choose that same day to go for a trail ride—and he happened to have a lariat along. When he came across a pretty damsel in distress in need of help, he did what any smart young cowboy would. He lowered his rope and brought her up to safety. He then did what any young cowboy worth his salt would *also* do and asked her out." He laughed softly at the memory. "The rest was history. Every significant moment in their life since happened in the mountains—he proposed to her on a ridgetop, they were married on another one. She used to say my name reminded her of all the happiest moments of her life and was a symbol of strength and invincibility."

She smiled, charmed by the sweetness of the story, until she remembered what had happened to that young couple.

"Your mother sounds…amazing," she murmured.

"She was," he said simply, then changed the subject with what she was certain was deliberate intent. "How's the arm? Do you need more of the pain meds?"

"Maybe just some ibuprofen. I think I had better take it easy on anything stronger. My head is spinning."

He crossed to the pitcher he had thoughtfully set out for her and poured a glass then brought it over to her, along with a couple of pills. For a gruff rancher, he seemed remarkably comfortable in the role of caregiver. She suspected raising a child probably contributed to that.

She wondered again about the girl's mother. Were they divorced or was he a widower? She wanted to ask but figured she had already filled her nervy quotient for a lifetime when it came to Ridge Bowman.

"I'm sorry I've been such a bother. I'll be out of the way in the morning."

She didn't want to feel this subtle connection to him. She would only find it that much harder to accept when he came to hate her after the truth came out.

"Are you supposed to be catching a flight back to San Diego in the next day or two? The way that snow is coming down, you might have a tough time making it to the airport, not to mention you might be a bit uncomfortable traveling with that broken arm for a day or two."

"My flight isn't until the end of the week. I had planned to stay in Pine Gulch through Christmas."

He looked surprised. "I thought you said you didn't have family around here."

"I don't," she answered. "Here, there or anywhere. Everyone's gone. My mother passed away two years ago and, as I told you, my father died earlier this year."

"You were an only child?"

"No," she said after a moment's hesitation. "I had an older brother but…he died twelve years ago."

She shouldn't have said that. She held her breath, afraid Ridge would probably find it an unusual coincidence that her older brother just happened to have died around the same time as his parents' murders.

She was beginning to suspect it wasn't a coincidence at all.

"So you were going to spend the holidays alone?" he asked.

"I've never minded my own company, Mr. Bowman."

"I enjoy mine, too. But not during the holidays."

He studied her for a long moment, and she had the odd impression he was weighing his words. "You could always spend the holidays here with Destry and me," he finally said slowly.

"What?" She blinked at him, certain she must have misheard.

"The inn is a great place, don't get me wrong. Not like it used to be, when nobody could recommend it. My sister-in-law Laura has worked hard to fix it up and all and make it a warm and welcoming hotel. But it's still a hotel, and you'd still be on your own. We'd love to have you here. As you can see, we've got plenty of room in this old place."

For a long moment, she fought a mix of shock, bemusement and a soft, sweet warmth. Was Ridge Bowman really asking a woman he had just met to spend the holidays at his ranch with him and his daughter?

"I…don't know what to say."

"You don't have to decide right this minute. It's the middle of the night. We both ought to be asleep. Good night."

He headed for the door, but she stopped him before he could reach it.

"Why would you make such an offer? You don't even know me. Why would you want a stranger to intrude in the middle of your family's holiday celebrations?"

He was quiet. "First of all, you wouldn't be intruding. When we were kids, we always had a houseful of people over for the holidays. My parents were known for throwing the River Bow open to anybody in need of a little holiday spirit. I guess in the past few years, we've kind of lost that along the way somehow."

"And?"

He scratched his cheek. "Well, you were hurt falling down my stairs. Seems to me, the least I can do is make you feel welcome here and give you a comfortable place to spend Christmas while you're recovering."

"You don't owe me anything," she exclaimed. "It was my own clumsiness."

"We do," he said. "Even if you hadn't been hurt here, there's the matter of the painting. You gave us

back something we thought was lost forever. I know my
brothers will want to meet you to thank you in person.
You might as well get used to the idea that the Bowman
family now owes you a debt and we always make good."

"I don't—"

"Just think about it. No rush. I'll check on you again
in a few hours when I head out to the barn. Meantime,
try to get some rest. We'll figure everything out in the
morning."

He gave her a lopsided smile, this big, rough cowboy she found so deeply attractive, then headed out of
the room with the little three-legged dog hopping along
behind him.

After he left, Sarah stared at the doorway, overwhelmed by his invitation.

She knew she shouldn't find the idea of staying in
this warm house for the holidays so very tempting. She
didn't belong here at the River Bow. Her whole presence
at the ranch had been a misjudgment on her part and a
case of mistaken identity on his.

No, she couldn't accept. She would have to simply make
her excuses in the morning and return to the Cold Creek
Inn—no matter how depressed that prospect left her.

Chapter Six

As predicted, the snow that had been lightly but steadily falling when he finally tumbled into bed the night before had become a full-on Rocky Mountain blizzard by morning.

After checking on his soundly sleeping guest and leaving a note for her outside her room where she couldn't help but see it, Ridge bundled into all his warmest gear and headed out into a miserable wind that blew ice into every available crevice.

At least a foot of snow had fallen during those few hours of restless sleep, and he couldn't see any sign of it easing up in the foreseeable future. He wouldn't be surprised if they had a good two feet for St. Nick and his reindeer to struggle through. Add in the wind that blew giant drifts to pile up in front of doorways and bury anything uncovered—like certain rental vehicles, for instance—and he didn't see how Sarah would have any other choice but to stay put on the River Bow for now.

He certainly wouldn't be able to take her anywhere for several hours. Most of his day would be spent digging out, clearing paths, repairing any damage from the winds.

Both of his brothers would probably be running all day responding to slide-offs and other weather-related issues in their respective emergency personnel modes, which meant that Destry would likely be stuck at Trace's house, too, at least until evening.

After a few hours of running the plow on the tractor—with many more to go—he decided to take a quick break. He needed more fuel than the quick cup of coffee and yogurt he had grabbed on his way out the door.

The contrast between the howling, bitter wind and the warmth of the mudroom was startling—and so was the tantalizing smell of frying bacon that drifted over him the moment he walked inside.

Hmm. Apparently his hunger was giving him aromatic hallucinations. There was a first.

By the time he shrugged out of his winter gear and walked into the kitchen, he discovered he wasn't imagining things.

Sarah stood at the stove, wearing a deep green robe that must have been one of Caidy's and an apron she must have found hanging in the pantry. Her casted arm looked pale and fragile in contrast.

"What's all this?" he demanded in surprise.

She flipped a strip of sizzling bacon in the pan. "Great timing, that's what it is. I woke up and saw you outside shoveling all that snow. When I came into the kitchen, I couldn't see any sign you'd had breakfast. I thought you might eventually come in to grab a bite so I started cooking. And here you are. I hope you don't mind."

He laughed. "Wrong question to ask a cowboy, if he minds somebody fixing him a meal. The answer to that question will always be no. I had resigned myself to a cold bowl of cereal so this is a great surprise. Just one question. How did you manage all this with a broken wing?"

"I would like to tell you it was easy, but that would be stretching the truth. The trickiest part was opening the bacon package, but somehow I managed."

She gave a rueful smile that completely charmed him—as if the breakfast wasn't enough on its own.

She scooped several perfectly crisp slices of bacon onto a plate and slid it across the island to him, followed by fluffy scrambled eggs and several pieces of toast. She dished out a much-smaller portion for herself.

He poured two glasses of juice from the refrigerator and then sat down across from her at the island, suddenly famished.

"Wow. This is delicious," he said after his first bite of eggs that were perfectly cooked. "Thank you."

She looked pleased. "You're welcome. I like to cook, even one-handed. I don't get the chance to do it for someone else very often."

"I don't mind cooking, either, when I have the time. Our parents made sure we all learned to fend for ourselves if we had to. I just rarely have the time—and I've never much needed to, with Caidy around. All that will change now. I'm looking to hire a housekeeper, but I figured I would wait until Destry and I have a chance to settle into a new routine and see what holes need filling."

"Is your sister moving far with her new husband?"

"Just a few miles away, actually. I imagine Caidy will take pity on us once in a while and throw a meal or two this direction, though she's got two stepchildren to take care of and a busy veterinarian for a husband."

She studied him while she ate a small forkful of scrambled eggs. "You're very close, aren't you?"

He sipped at his juice, remembering how radiant his baby sister had looked when he gave her away. Out of nowhere, he felt a little melancholy. All his siblings were moving on with their lives while he was here shoveling the same damn driveway, repairing the same damn barn roof.

"Hard not to be," he answered. "Caidy has been helping me out with my daughter since Destry was in diapers. We would have been lost without her after my wife took off."

Now why the hell had he told her that? Ridge set down his fork, losing a little of his appetite despite the delicious breakfast. He rarely talked about Melinda anymore. What was the point? Yet here he was blurting out the pleasant news that she had left him alone with a young baby.

"What a loving sister," she murmured.

He found himself unexpectedly amused that she had jumped there instead of the obvious.

"You're not going to ask why my wife left? Seems to me, that would be an irresistible follow-up question for most women I know."

She shrugged as much as she could with one arm in a sling. "I assumed if you wanted me to know, you would have finished the sentence. 'We would have been lost without her after my wife took off to swallow flaming knives with the circus. After my wife took off to become a Radio City Music Hall dancer. After my wife took off to shave her head and join a cult.' That sort of thing."

His burst of laughter seemed to surprise both of them. He tried to picture Melinda shaving her head and couldn't quite pull it off. "Any of those answers would be more interesting than the bare-bones truth. She didn't like ranch life. She hated the wind and the flies and the dirt."

And me, he wanted to add. By the time Melinda walked out, she had hated Ridge for refusing to leave the ranch and had accused him of loving the River Bow more than he loved her. By that point, he had.

"She left her daughter because of that? Her daughter and the, er, man she loved?"

He wanted to think she had loved him once, but he wasn't sure anymore. "We weren't a very good mix from the get-go. And I think some people make choices they later come to regret. All these years, I thought she just abandoned our daughter, but this year I finally had a private investigator search for her and discovered she died about a year after she took off. I like to think she would have reconsidered and tried to reconnect with Des. Guess we'll never know for sure."

"That must be hard on your daughter."

He was touched by her compassion for a girl she didn't even know. Maybe it stemmed from being an educator.

"You know, she's an amazingly well-adjusted young lady. With Caidy's help and the rest of the family's, I think we've managed to do a pretty good job of giving her all the love she needs to thrive, even without a mother."

"She's lucky to have you all," Sarah said softly.

"We're lucky to have each other," he said. "My brothers and their families still come home just about every week for Sunday dinner, though we decided to take a pass this week given the wedding on Friday and Christmas in only a few days. We are getting together for Christmas dinner this week. You'll have a chance to meet them all then."

"About that—" she began.

He knew she was going to argue about staying through Christmas and he suddenly didn't want her to.

"They're going to be so happy to see the painting. I was telling my brother Trace about it last night. We're both really curious about how your father might have come into possession of it."

An odd spark flashed in her eyes, almost like fear, but she quickly looked down at her plate. "I'm...not sure," she said. "To be honest, I didn't know my father well. We were virtual strangers most of my life."

"Oh?"

She sighed. "My parents divorced when I was five and he took custody of my brother, who was several years older than I was. They lived mostly in Las Vegas and rarely came to the coast. I had maybe two mandated weeks with him in the summers and not even that, most of the time. I had little to do with him after I turned eighteen, by my own choice."

"Divorce can be tough on kids." He had a very strong suspicion she didn't talk about this very often, and he was touched that she was willing to discuss it with him. Something about the wind howling under the eaves and the snow falling heavily outside and the homey morning breakfast smells lent a quiet intimacy to the warmth of the kitchen that invited confidences.

"I see that with my students," she answered. "It's only natural for young children to feel like they're responsible somehow. And situations where children are split up between parents can add a special kind of hell to a child's psyche. For a long time, I couldn't understand what I had done wrong that he didn't want me but he wanted Joey. My mother was…bitter about the divorce and the reasons that led up to it. And you know how some people are quietly bitter? That wasn't my mother. By the time they finally divorced, she hated my father, and her anger sat at the dinner table with us every night. She hated that he refused to change, even for her. She always said—"

She broke off the words and suddenly bit her lip. "Sorry. I don't know why I'm rambling on like this. Why should you care about my boring dysfunctional family? Can I get you more bacon?"

She jumped up from the table. In her rush, she moved too quickly and wobbled a little to regain her equilibrium. Out of instinct, he jumped up to catch her before she fell or bumped her arm.

They froze that way, with her arms against his chest and his on her upper arms. She looked up at him, eyes huge. He saw her throat move as she swallowed, and he could swear her gaze flickered to his mouth.

Heat surged through him, wild and urgent. He wanted to kiss her, with an ache that shocked the hell out of him. She felt perfect in his arms, soft and warm, and he knew it was crazy but all he could think about was leaning down, brushing his mouth against hers, tasting those incredibly soft-looking lips….

She barely knew him, he reminded himself. They were alone in his house. Beyond that, she was stranded here, at least for now. He wouldn't take advantage of that and probably completely freak her out by kissing her out of the blue.

He drew on every ounce of self-control hard-won over the past ten years to keep the embrace impersonally helpful instead of yanking her against him as he wanted to do.

"You okay now?"

A very adorable pink blush stained her cheeks. "I... think so. I must have stood up too fast."

"Not to mention, you pushed yourself too hard making breakfast this morning, considering you broke a bone twenty-four hours ago and you've still probably got pain medication on board."

"I'm sure that's true."

What the hell was wrong with him? She was injured and hurting, and all he wanted to do was kiss away that soft, sweet brush of color on her cheekbones.

"You can let go now," she murmured after another moment. "I think I'm okay."

"You sure? This tile floor is pretty hard. Doc Dalton might wonder what's going on out here if you took a header and cracked your head open, too."

"I would tell him it's only me and my usual clumsiness."

She smiled, and he couldn't seem to look away. Almost against his will, he leaned down just a little. He saw her breath catch, saw her eyes widen. Her mouth parted, and he knew he didn't misinterpret the way she leaned toward him, ever so slightly.

A particularly strong gust of wind rattled the windows in the kitchen, and the sound was enough to yank him back to his senses.

With no small amount of regret, he eased his arms

away slowly to make sure she wasn't going to teeter again.

"I hate to leave you, but do you think you'll be okay in here without me for a while? Except for the wind, it looks like the snow is easing up a little. I should really go out and hit the plow again. I might be able to clear the driveway enough for Destry to make it back before dinner."

"I should be fine," she said, quickly veiling her expression, but not before he saw what looked like a little glint of disappointment. "In fact, if your daughter is able to make it out to the ranch, there shouldn't be any reason why I can't go back in the other direction and return to the inn."

He wanted to argue and invite her again to stay at the ranch for the holidays—but given his crazy response to her, maybe that wasn't the best idea.

"We'll see. Take it easy and get some rest. Let's see how you feel this afternoon."

He headed for the mudroom and his winter gear. For once he figured he would welcome the blast of cold air. He needed *something* to cool his fevered thoughts.

As soon as she heard the door close behind Ridge, Sarah covered her overheated cheeks with her palms.

Wow. What just happened?

For a moment there, she had been certain he would kiss her. Had it all been some pain reliever–induced figment of her imagination? No. She couldn't claim to be the most experienced woman on the planet, but he had most definitely leaned closer, until she thought she could feel his heartbeat pulse against her.

What would she have done? She certainly wouldn't

have resisted. She had *wanted* him to kiss her, had ached for it. Her own heartbeat had been racing in her ears and her nerves had shivered in anticipation.

She was fiercely attracted to him, more than she had ever been attracted to anyone in her life. She frowned, astonished at herself and her reaction. This just wasn't like her.

She certainly dated in San Diego and had come close to being engaged to a highly successful attorney, until her mother's debilitating stroke. Michael hadn't been at all supportive during those long months of stress. He resented the hours she felt obligated to stay with her mother at the care center, as Barbara's only living relative. Until then, she had never realized how inherently selfish he was, in that and many other ways. Seeing him filtered through the different light of her own stressful situation made her grateful she hadn't yet agreed to marry him. Breaking up after two years of exclusive dating had been more relief than heartbreak.

Probably because of the comfortable placidity of her near engagement, she found this wild attraction to Ridge Bowman new and disturbing.

This place was to blame, she decided. She hadn't been herself since she showed up at the River Bow. She had this strange sense of belonging here, of homecoming, that made absolutely no sense.

She needed to push that right out of her head. She didn't belong here—and the next time she was tempted to kiss the man, she needed to remember what would happen when Ridge found out the truth. He certainly wouldn't want her in his arms—or anywhere near his ranch or his daughter.

Fighting off a lingering depression, she stood and

began to clear the few breakfast dishes to tidy up. She was loading the last dish in the dishwasher when a familiar ringtone rang through the kitchen. Her phone! He must have found it in the car after all.

The ringing stopped by the time she made it to her purse and pawed through with one hand for her phone—which was much more difficult than she might have expected.

When she recognized her best friend Nicole's name on the recent-call log, she briefly entertained the idea of ignoring it, but perhaps a connection to her regular life might keep her anchored in reality, she thought.

Anyway, Nicki would probably keep calling until she picked up. Her impatient college roommate had always been that way.

She quickly dialed her back. While she waited for Nicki to pick up, she tried to formulate how much she could possibly tell her about the past twenty-four hours.

"There you are! I thought maybe you dropped off the face of the earth," Nicki exclaimed with the gerbil-on-crack energy and enthusiasm that always made Sarah smile.

She always figured the gods of college roommates had been particularly kind the day the two of them had been assigned together freshman year at UCLA. Where Sarah tended to be reserved and cautious, Nicki barged into every situation at full tilt. They had been BFFs since the very first day on campus, when they had stayed up all night exchanging life stories.

"I'm still here."

"Where? I ran by your condo last night, and you weren't home. I stopped again this morning, and you still weren't there. I've got to tell you, my imagination is in overdrive, wondering if you're with some hot guy you didn't tell me about."

She flushed and looked out the window, where she could see the outline of a certain extremely hot rancher shoveling his sidewalk.

Nicki knew more than anyone about her tangled family connections—it was hard to avoid telling her when they had lived together for all four years of school—but Sarah hadn't told her what she found in that storage unit or about her impromptu trip to Eastern Idaho.

"Why the urgency?" she asked, avoiding the question. "What's up?"

"Oh, you know. This and that. Okay, the truth is I have news. *Huge* news. But I don't want to tell you over the phone. Wherever you are, meet me in an hour at the Fishwife for brunch so I can spill."

She sighed, looking out at the vast expanse of mountains and snow out the window, which seemed far away from their favorite beachside restaurant.

"I'm sorry, hon. I can't. I'm afraid you'll have to tell me over the phone. I just had breakfast."

Nicole made a disappointed sound. "Lunch, then. Or coffee. Or pie. I don't care what. I want to see your face when I tell you."

"Does this have anything to do with the certain junior high science teacher you've been dating and perhaps any emotionally and socially significant gifts of jewelry that might have been offered and accepted?"

Nicole snorted. "Forget it. You're not going to break me that easily with your smarty-pants teacher talk. I won't spoil the surprise until I can squeal and hug my maid of honor in person. Just tell me where you are and I'll come to you."

"Doesn't it count if I squeal over the phone and give you a virtual hug?"

"No!" Nicki exclaimed. "Where the heck are you?"

She sighed. Like it or not, she was going to have to tell her friend and deal with the fallout. "I'm sorry, Nic. You know I would be there in a minute to celebrate with you if I could, but I can't. I should have told you, but to be fair, it was a last-minute decision, and anyway, I thought you were going to be spending the holidays in Big Bear with Jason's family."

"Told me what?"

"I'm in Idaho."

A long, echoing silence met her words.

"Excuse me. We must have a bad connection. Did you just say…Idaho."

"Erm, yes."

"As in potatoes."

She had to smile, as she hadn't seen a single tuber since she arrived two days earlier. "Yes. Actually, I'm almost to the Wyoming border. A little town called Pine Gulch."

"And the rest of the story is…"

"Long and complicated. Too long and complicated for me to adequately explain over the phone. I'm so sorry I'm not there to celebrate with the two of you, Nic. I really am."

"You're going to leave me hanging like that? So unfair."

"This, from the woman who won't even tell me she's engaged unless we're face-to-face?"

"How do you know whether I'm engaged or not? That's purely speculative."

She laughed, deeply grateful for one of the people she

loved most in the world. "You're right. I know nothing. I'm probably way off base anyway."

"And I know less than nothing about what you're doing there." Nicole paused. "Wait. Does this have anything to do with your father?"

She shivered a little at her friend's unerring guess. Nicole didn't know the full story of Vasily Malikov's criminal background—not that Sarah did, either—but she had shared enough details over the years with her friend that she could probably guess. Nicole certainly knew Sarah was left with the difficult task of trying to settle his complicated affairs.

She didn't want to talk about her family, so she chose the best method of distraction she could think of on short notice—which happened to be at the forefront of her brain because it was beginning to throb incessantly.

"Oh, I almost forgot to tell you," she said. "When I get back to San Diego, I'm going to have to take a rain check on our Saturday-morning tennis matches for a while. I, um, sort of broke my arm yesterday."

"What?" Nicole exclaimed. "What *else* haven't you told me? Have you got a new husband you haven't bothered to mention? And how does somebody *sort of* break an arm?"

"Okay. I broke my arm. No *sort of* about it. It is a clean break though, apparently, and I should be okay in about four weeks. No surgery necessary. And no new husband, believe me."

To her relief, Nicole let herself be distracted instead of pushing for further explanations about her father and her presence in Pine Gulch, answers Sarah wasn't yet ready to provide.

"Oh, you poor thing! Who's taking care of you? Do

you know somebody there in this Pine Gulch? Let me come get you and take you home where you belong. I'll skip Big Bear. Jason's family will understand."

Her friend's concern somehow made her feel much better about things.

"You know, I think I'll be okay. People here have been very kind. I've even had an invitation to spend Christmas with some people I've met here, and I'm seriously considering taking it."

It was a lie, but she could sort it out with Nicole over waffles at the Fishwife when she returned.

"I wish you would tell me what's going on," her friend said, obvious concern in her voice.

"I will. And please tell a certain seventh-grade science teacher, who might or might not be engaged, congratulations for me. He's the luckiest man I know."

"You promise you'll spill everything?"

"Pinkie promise."

"And you're safe? People are taking care of you?"

"I'm fine, honey. You go to Big Bear and have a wonderful time. Do me a favor, though. Be careful and don't break any bones. I can promise, it's not a great way to spend the holidays."

Nicole reluctantly hung up a short time later. After she disconnected, Sarah sat for a moment in the big, comfortable kitchen, listening to the house settle around her.

Without Ridge's conversation or Nicole's cheerful chatter on the phone, her own company somehow seemed unsettling. At loose ends, she wandered into the great room, dominated by that massive Christmas tree and the festive greenery all around.

Ridge hadn't turned on any of the Christmas lights

before he headed outside to shovel. Though it was late morning already, the day outside was still heavy and dark from the storm and the endless wind. On impulse, she searched until she found a switch. The Christmas tree lights came on as well as the little fairy lights nestled in the greenery above the fireplace and trailing up the staircase.

Immediately, her mood lightened.

She had the oddest feeling in this house. She didn't understand it and assumed it had to be the lingering effects from the pain medication. Nothing else explained why she felt this overwhelming sense of warmth and welcome here, why the very walls of the log ranch house seemed to be urging her to settle in and be comfortable.

She loved her own condo just a few blocks from the ocean and had worked two jobs for a long time to save for the down payment, but she wasn't sure she ever felt the same sense of cozy contentment there.

A picture above the mantel drew her gaze, and she saw it was a mountain scene, with horses in the foreground who looked as if they could run off the painting, and a compelling old cabin with weathered log walls and fluttery lace curtains.

Even before she saw the flowing signature of Margaret Bowman, she knew by the style and skillful use of color and perspective that it must have been painted by Ridge's mother.

That alone was enough to remind her she *didn't* belong here. Like the painting, the feeling was only an artful illusion, and she would do well to remember that.

Chapter Seven

He stayed out in the cold for several hours, plowing neighbors' driveways and digging out mailboxes buried by blowing snowdrifts and the county road crews.

The heater in the tractor cab had stopped working about an hour earlier and he was chilled to the bone. Though the snow had stopped for now, the clouds were heavy and dark, and he expected several more inches would fall overnight.

As Ridge finally drove the tractor up the long, curving lane that led from Cold Creek Road to the ranch house, nestled in the trees, he was greeted by a scene that belonged on a greeting card.

There, shining through the gloom, was the house where he had lived most of his life, the front window gleaming with color and light from the huge Christmas tree Caidy and Destry had spent the entire Thanksgiving weekend decorating.

He stopped the tractor and just savored the view. He loved this place, every last inch of it. The house, the barn, the outbuildings, the acreage. He knew it as well as he knew his own face in the mirror.

His houseguest must have turned on the tree lights. He wondered how she was doing and hoped she had found the chance to rest. Guilt pinched at him, knowing he had left her far too long. He should have checked on her an hour ago.

He meant to earlier, but time had this bad habit of slipping away from him. He could also be honest enough with himself to admit he was also a little leery about facing her again after that moment when he had nearly kissed her in the kitchen.

That hadn't stopped him from thinking about her all afternoon. She was hiding something from him. He was certain of it, though he couldn't have said why.

Hell, he'd only met the woman a little more than twenty-four hours earlier. He didn't really know anything about her, other than that she was lovely as a spring meadow, that she didn't have anywhere else to go for the holidays and that she made him begin to crave all these crazy things he never thought he needed.

Despite their short acquaintance, he still sensed secrets seething beneath her outward calm like rainbow trout darting around under the ice of Cold Creek. He wanted to dip his hand in and catch a few of them.

After enjoying the view for a few more moments, he drove up to the house and parked close. Broken heater or not, he was going to have to go out to plow again before the storm blew itself out and passed away from Pine Gulch. It was an inevitable part of wintertime here on the western slope of the Tetons.

When he walked into the mudroom, he was again met by something tantalizing, rich and hearty. His stomach growled in a rather embarrassing way. He took off his winter clothes and walked in to find an empty kitchen. One of Caidy's slow cookers steamed on the countertop.

Though his sister had often instructed him on the cardinal rule of slow cookers—don't lift the lid!—he was too curious, and, hey, male. He couldn't resist doing just that. To his amazed delight, he discovered one of his very favorite winter meals: a beef stew brimming with onions, potatoes and carrots.

His houseguest must have thrown it together. How had she managed to peel and slice the vegetables with a broken arm?

A warmth that had nothing to do with the furnace seeped through him. After another quick, appreciative sniff, he closed the lid and went in search of her.

He found her snuggled up under a blanket on one of the sofas in the great room, positioned so she could see both the blazing Christmas tree and the fire that sizzled and hummed in the river-rock fireplace.

He opened his mouth to greet her, then realized her eyes were closed, her breathing even. A strand of auburn hair drifted across her cheek and he had to clench a fist to keep from pushing it back.

She looked so peaceful there, lovely and sweet and more relaxed than he had seen her since she arrived at the ranch.

Despite his better instincts, Ridge indulged his cold, achy bones and sank down onto the other sofa. He had a million things to do. Running a cattle ranch left him very little leisure time. He could always find some task to fill his downtime—ranch accounts, ordering supplies, tinkering with the stupid heater on the John Deere.

He hadn't slept much the night before. Just for a moment, he decided to sit by his own fire on a cold, snowy afternoon and relax while the Christmas lights flickered on the tree.

The past week revving up to the wedding had been so crazy, he hadn't had a single moment of downtime. As he sat there with the fire warming his feet, tension he hadn't even been aware of began to trickle away. He exhaled heavily and closed his eyes—just for a moment, he told himself.

Sometime later, the sound of the front door slamming pierced through a hazy, delicious dream that involved a lovely woman with auburn hair and blue-gray eyes and a soft, eager mouth...

"Dad! I'm home!"

He jerked back to full awareness just as his daughter bolted in at full tilt, like a gawky energetic colt.

He blinked a few times. Surely he hadn't been asleep. He *never* took naps. But the fire had burned down and his eyes felt heavy and swollen, so he must have been out for a while.

For a moment, Destry looked mildly surprised to find him sitting on the living room sofa, apparently doing nothing. "Hi, Dad!" she exclaimed.

"Hey there," he said softly. He quickly rose and headed back to the foyer so their guest could keep sleeping.

Destry followed him, dropping her backpack on a chair as she went. "You wouldn't believe the crazy roads. Uncle Trace had to drive like two miles an hour all the way here."

"Is that so?" he murmured softly as Trace walked in carrying an unfamiliar suitcase, Gabi right behind him hauling a mysterious plastic bin whose contents he couldn't discern.

"I didn't think I would see you guys today. I figured you wouldn't be able to make it through the snow."

"You got a lot more out here than we did in town, and we didn't have the wind," his brother said. "Anyway, what's a blizzard when you've got four-wheel drive and a couple of determined girls on your hands?"

Gabi and Destry both giggled, something they tended to do a great deal of whenever they were together. He never minded it. What else were girls their age supposed to do?

"Sorry to make you drive me home in the snow, Uncle Trace," Destry said. "I just have *so* much to do before Christmas, you know? We've only got *two days*. Can you believe it? Now that we finished the, er, things we were making at your place, I wanted to come home to finish the rest. I didn't want you out here by yourself, now that Aunt Caidy's on her honeymoon."

"I'm not by myself," he started to explain, but at that moment, Destry's attention was caught by something in the living room. Sarah, he realized. She had sat up and was looking around the room sleepily, her hair messed up from sleeping on her side.

She looked completely delectable, especially when she flushed a little to find them all looking at her.

"Oh. Hi."

Her voice sounded husky with sleep, and Ridge had to swallow hard at the instant heat that surged through him.

He did his best to ignore the arched eyebrow Trace

sent his way. Sometimes younger brothers were a pain in the ass.

"Sorry we woke you," he said. "Look who showed up. This is my brother Trace, my daughter, Destry, and Trace's sister-in-law, Gabi. Everybody, this is Sarah Whitmore."

Sarah tucked her feet under the blanket. "Hi," she said with a nervous sort of smile. His family could be overwhelming. At least she was meeting them a few at a time.

"Hi, Sarah," Gabi said cheerfully. "Did you really break your arm falling down the stairs?"

Sarah lifted her cast, her expression embarrassed. "Can you believe anybody would be so clumsy?"

"Does it hurt a lot?" Gabi asked. "I sprained my wrist one time playing dodgeball at school, and it hurt like *crazy.* I couldn't use it for like two weeks. I had a cast and everything. It did help me get out of like four tests, since I couldn't write the answers, so that was kind of awesome."

"So that's why you didn't complain more about your injury," Trace said, rolling his eyes at his young sister-in-law. Gabi was quite a character, someone who had grown up learning how to manipulate circumstances to her advantage. "All this time, I thought you were just being brave."

"I was! It still hurt like crazy."

Trace laughed and nudged her with his shoulder. He loved the girl like a daughter, something that warmed Ridge to see.

He didn't look quite as favorably on his brother when Trace turned his attention to Sarah.

"Ridge was telling me last night about the painting

you brought with you to Pine Gulch. He said you wanted to give it back to the family."

"Er, yes. That's the plan." She looked down at her hands, clearly uncomfortable at the direction the conversation had taken.

"That seems like quite a remarkably generous gesture. It's not a masterpiece by any means, but it's still a valuable painting, especially given the history. Were you aware our mother's work is beginning to fetch in the five figures?"

"I can certainly see why," she murmured, gesturing to one of Ridge's favorites on the mantel, one of her earlier works they had been able to purchase a few years ago. "She was very gifted."

"But you still want to give it to us. Complete strangers."

She sent a fleeting glance in Ridge's direction, and her cheeks colored, which he interpreted to mean she didn't consider him a *complete* stranger. Good thing, especially since he'd nearly kissed her a few hours earlier.

"Keeping it wouldn't have been right. The painting never belonged to me," she said quietly. "I'm not sure how my father obtained it, but it appears your family has rightful claim to it. Especially given that history you referred to."

"That's quite an unusual position to take. I'm not sure many people would agree. Possession being nine-tenths of the law in many people's minds."

"I'm sure you would agree, Chief Bowman, that legalities and moralities are sometimes two very different things."

She said the words in that same even tone, and Trace

studied her carefully as if he were weighing every syllable, every expression.

Ridge could tell Sarah was growing increasingly uncomfortable, and he found himself wanting to tell his brother to back the hell off.

"And you really have no idea how or where your father obtained it?" Trace pushed.

"I was estranged from my father for many years before his death."

"And yet he left you what could be a valuable painting."

"Yes," she said, her voice tight, and Ridge had had enough.

"It's in my office. Come on back and take a look."

He said the words in a firm command his brother couldn't mistake.

After a moment, Trace followed him down the hall with clear reluctance. Ridge could tell his brother wanted to push harder for information on the painting's journey into her father's possession, but he wasn't about to let him badger Sarah.

His protective impulse toward her both surprised and alarmed him, but he told himself he would do the same for anybody.

The painting still held a place of honor on the credenza. He saw exactly the moment Trace caught sight of it. His brother's rugged features softened with raw emotion, and he moved to stand directly in front of it. He touched a finger to the edge of the frame as if he couldn't quite believe they had this piece of her back, after all these years.

"I remember the day Mom started this one," he said, his voice low. "We all went for a picnic up by Winder

Lake one evening. Do you remember? Taft and I were probably still single digits. You were maybe twelve. You and Dad and Taft went off fishing, but I had a stomach-ache and I think I was pissed at Taft for something, as usual, so I stuck with Mom and Caidy."

He paused, his fingers tracing one of the brush marks. "I watched her do a bunch of sketches of Caidy that looked just like this, only more raw. She also did a few of me, as I recall. It was always kind of a miracle to me how she could make somebody come alive on paper with only a pencil."

"She definitely had a gift. Too bad she didn't pass it down to any of us."

"I'm hoping my son will inherit it. He might only be six months old but I'm telling you, he has a great eye for color."

Ridge smiled at the obvious love in Trace's voice whenever he spoke about Will or about Gabi. It was a little odd seeing both of his brothers in these family roles, but he was exceptionally proud of the fathers they had become, probably because they had a damn good example in Frank Bowman.

It was kind of funny that both of the wild twins had settled down to become family men. Trace and his wife, Becca, had taken on responsibility for Gabi before they were married, while Taft had just a year ago formally adopted his wife Laura's two children from her first marriage, the mischievous and energetic Alex and darling little Maya.

"Caidy is going to cry buckets when she sees this. You know that, right?"

"Oh, yeah. At least two or three. I thought maybe

the three of us could give it to her for a belated wedding gift."

"That's a great idea," Trace said. "I'm sure Taft will agree."

"It's good to have it back, isn't it? Admit it."

His brother frowned. "I never said it wasn't. I'm as happy to see it again as you are. But if we knew more about how this woman's father came into possession of a hot painting, we might be a step closer to cracking the case and bringing their killers to justice. Even a tiny clue—a name, a receipt, a wire transfer—could lead us in a new direction."

Trace had never given up his quest to find the murderers. Ridge knew how important that was to his brother, partly because of the role Becca's mother played in the crime. From what little they could piece together, Trace's witch of a mother-in-law had been involved in reconnaissance for the planned art thefts that had unexpectedly turned into a double murder when the Bowmans had surprised the thieves by being home.

Unfortunately, the investigation into the crime stalled after Monica claimed she didn't know who else had been involved. Ridge knew it chafed Trace that he hadn't been able to interrogate the woman further about the crimes. Instead, he had been forced to make the difficult choice of letting Monica go free in exchange for her agreement to sign over permanent custody of Gabi to Becca.

Under the circumstances, he had to respect the decision Trace had made, choosing an innocent young girl's future happiness over his own burning desire for vengeance. He understood and probably would have made the same choice.

While he sympathized with Trace's frustration after

twelve years of dead ends, he wasn't about to let him harass Sarah in his search for those answers.

"She said she doesn't know, and I want you to leave it at that," he said firmly.

"She might know more than she's telling you. Even more than she *thinks* she knows. Sometimes it just takes the right question to bring out unexpected answers."

"Back off," he warned, his voice hard. While his younger brother might be chief of police in Pine Gulch, Ridge still considered himself in charge when it came to matters here at the ranch. And since Sarah was his guest, she was also his responsibility. "I don't want you hounding her about this, you hear me? She's a nice woman, who has done an amazingly generous thing to return the painting to us."

"Maybe it's the cop in me but I don't trust that kind of unprovoked altruism."

He snorted. "She teaches first grade, Trace. She's not some kind of a criminal mastermind. Seriously, let it go."

Trace looked as if he wanted to argue, but he finally shrugged. "You want to take things at face value, fine. I'll let it go. For now."

Ridge supposed he would have to be content with that. "So tell me what Destry and Gabi have been up to."

"Beats the hell out of me. Everybody at my house seems to be keeping secrets right now, even Gabi's ugly dog."

That made two of them, Ridge thought. Apparently there were secrets to spare right now, and he had a feeling not all of them had to do with Christmas surprises.

Sarah fought down her dismay and fear while Ridge and his brother walked out of the room.

She had no idea how to deal with a hard-looking police chief who looked at her with suspicion and mistrust.

Could she be charged with possession of stolen property? She would have to talk to the estate attorney about that.

Abruptly, anger sizzled through the panic. She was furious suddenly at her father for leaving her to clean up this mess.

She ought to just tell Ridge everything. About her father, about Joe. She didn't want to believe it, but she was becoming increasingly convinced her brother had something to do with the Bowman murders.

It couldn't be a coincidence that he died only a few hundred miles from here, just a few days after the murders. That storage unit full of paintings was further proof. Her father must have been involved somehow. The Malikov crime family had probably orchestrated the whole thing—which still made her wonder why her father had never tried to liquidate the art.

How could she tell Ridge about her family background? He would despise her if he knew even a fraction of what she came from. He would no doubt see the daughter of a Russian organized crime figure as something foreign and undesirable.

She would tell him before she left, she promised herself, when she wouldn't have to face the condemnation in his green eyes.

The deception by omission didn't sit comfortably with her, but she pushed it away. Instead, she turned to the two young girls who were watching her with wary curiosity.

"I have to tell you, that Christmas tree is just about

the prettiest one I've ever seen, Destry. Did you help decorate it?"

"Yeah. It took me and my aunt Caidy like two whole days by the time we finished hanging all the decorations. That doesn't count all the time making some and buying others."

"It's really lovely. The whole house is the perfect Christmas home."

"It is pretty cool during the holidays," Destry agreed. "We go cut our own tree up in the mountains right before Thanksgiving. And sometimes my dad hitches up the wagon to the horses, and we go for sleigh rides up and down the road singing Christmas carols."

"That sounds really wonderful."

"I'm sorry you were hurt at our house. How did you fall down the stairs?"

"I wasn't paying attention to where I was walking, I guess. As a result, I missed a step and lost my balance."

"I do that all the time," Gabi assured her. "Trace says I'm always in too big of a hurry and I need to slow down."

"That's probably very good advice. I'll try to work on that. But, really, I'm fine. I've been trying to convince your father, Destry, that I'll be okay back at the inn where I've been staying. So far I haven't had much luck."

"He can be pretty stubborn," the girl said, fully in sympathy. "I've been wanting to start wearing makeup and pierce my ears for like *ages,* and he won't listen. I think he wishes we were pioneers or Amish or something. Becca lets Gabi wear lip gloss and eye shadow. I don't know why I can't."

She didn't feel qualified to comment and decided

to head off the insurrection before it could gather any steam.

"So what's in the box?"

Destry let herself be distracted easily. "A present for my dad," she said, her features bright. "You should see it. It's going to be *awesome*."

"No doubt," she said.

"Show her," Gabi urged.

Destry appeared to hesitate.

"You don't have to show me if you don't want to," Sarah assured her.

"You can't say anything. I want him to be totally surprised."

"My lips are sealed, I swear."

Destry set the box on the sofa beside Sarah and pulled open the lid. Almost reverently, she pulled out a nearly finished throw blanket in shades of brown and green.

"Wow," she exclaimed, impressed. "You made that? Seriously?"

"My aunt Becca taught me to knit. I'm still not very good but I've been working on it for like *weeks*. Last week I realized there was no *way* I would be done in time for Christmas unless I hauled some serious butt, so that's what we've been doing. My fingers literally feel like they're going to fall off."

"He'll love it," Sarah assured her. "Especially because you went to all the trouble to make it."

"I hope so. I dropped a lot of stitches. Aunt Becca was going to show me how to finish it but the baby was being kind of cranky this weekend and she didn't have a chance."

Sarah hesitated, torn between her natural teacher instincts and desire to help and her fear that the more enmeshed she became in the Bowmans' lives, the more difficult it would be to say goodbye to them all.

If she were smart, she would ask Trace Bowman to take her back to the Cold Creek Inn, but she really didn't want to spend more time with the police chief than she absolutely had to. She could spend one more night here, she decided, then drive back herself the next morning.

"I can knit. I'm not super great, either—and now I've only got one hand—but maybe between the two of us, we can figure things out."

"Really? That would be great! Thank you!"

"No problem," she said.

Male voices suddenly heralded the return of Ridge and his brother, and the girls rushed to close the plastic bin before either could sneak a peek.

When the men returned, Sarah tensed, waiting for the police chief to recommence his interrogation. If he did, she would have to tell them all the truth far earlier than she wanted. Unlike the rest of her family, she had never been good at lies or subterfuge.

To her vast relief, Chief Bowman didn't comment again on the painting.

"The snow is starting up again so we should probably start heading back, Gabs. We don't want to be stuck out here on the ranch. I don't know about you, but I wouldn't like to feel Becca's wrath if I have to leave her alone much longer with a cranky baby."

The girl rose. "Okay. See you, Uncle Ridge. Bye, Des. Ms. Whitmore, it was nice to meet you. I'm really sorry about your arm."

"Thank you."

When the two of them left, Sarah suddenly remembered the slow cooker meal she had thrown together before she came back into the great room and fell asleep by the fireplace.

"Are you hungry?" she asked. "I made stew earlier."

"It smells delicious. You mind if I wait awhile? I should probably go try to take a look at the heater on the tractor while I've still got a little daylight. Will you two be okay in here if I head out?"

Destry gave Sarah a sidelong, secretive look. "Go ahead. We'll be just fine," she said, with just a tad too much enthusiasm in her voice.

Ridge looked a little confused but apparently decided to let it go. "Call me if you have any problems. I don't know how late I'll be so go ahead and eat without me."

"Sure," Destry said.

He headed for the kitchen. As soon as they heard the door close, she and Destry went to work.

Chapter Eight

Apparently she had led a safe, sheltered life in San Diego. She had absolutely no idea until now that snow could fall with such relentless abandon.

A few hours later, Sarah sat at the kitchen table at the River Bow, Tripod at her feet, watching Destry roll out bread sticks from dough she had mixed up herself—apparently one of the specialties she had learned from her aunt.

"I can never make them look even," Destry complained. "My aunt Caidy's really good at it but mine are always bulgy on one side, no matter how careful I am. Not that it really matters. My dad eats them anyway, bulgy or not."

Sarah smiled, though she couldn't help searching out the window for further sign of him. He had been gone a long time. Destry seemed unconcerned, but Sarah couldn't help watching for him—despite the fact that she couldn't see more than a few feet past the window.

She had certainly seen news coverage of bad storms that socked in entire states, had read about them in books. But growing up in the mild, constant climate in San Diego hadn't prepared her at all for the raw ferocity of a heavy low-pressure system. What had always seemed a rather abstract concept to her was quickly becoming cold, blowing reality that went on and on.

She wouldn't be going back to town that evening, and possibly not the next.

She knew that should probably upset her but despite her worry for Ridge she had enjoyed the afternoon in the cozy, warm ranch house immensely.

With a fire merrily burning in the great-room hearth, she and Destry had worked together to finish the knitted throw. Sarah was far from an expert, but she had enjoyed teaching the girl. The result was a beautiful blanket that she knew Ridge would cherish, especially knowing his daughter had worked so hard on it.

"We just need to let these rise for a half hour and then we can throw them in the oven," Destry said.

"They look absolutely beautiful. I can't wait to try them."

The girl grinned at her and set the jelly roll pan of bread sticks on the countertop.

"Hey, you want some hot cocoa? My aunt Caidy has like twenty different mixes, and I think she left most of them. Mint chocolate, orange chocolate, caramel chocolate. Whatever you want. She orders them from some fancy gourmet coffee place in Jackson Hole."

"Which one is best?"

"They're all good but I think raspberry is my favorite."

"Sure. Raspberry sounds great. Can I help?"

Destry made a face. "No. If I were making it the hard way, with fresh cream and shaved chocolate and stuff, I might need help, but this is super easy. All you have to do is heat up the water in the microwave, add the mix and you're set."

The hard way sounded absolutely divine, and she vowed to get the recipe from Destry before she returned to San Diego, but right now raspberry cocoa from a mix would be great. She rose to grab four ibuprofen for her aching arm from the bottle by the sink, poured a glass of water and swallowed just as a particularly hard gust of wind hurled flakes against the window and rattled the glass.

She shivered. "Will your dad be okay out there?"

Destry followed her gaze out the window at the swirling, unceasing snow. "He's a rancher. He's used to bad weather. It's part of the life," she said simply.

Sarah considered that quite an insight from a girl who was not yet twelve. "Will he be able to come in for dinner?"

Destry nodded. "Oh, I'm sure he'll come in soon to eat. He usually does. Sometimes he goes back out after dinner, but with this much snow, he might call it a night and start again first thing in the morning."

Their lifestyle was as foreign to Sarah as a Kabuki dancer's but she found a rhythm and peace in it that called to her.

"Do you like growing up on a ranch?" she asked Destry.

Destry furrowed her brow as if she'd never considered the question before. "Sure I do. I mean, what's not to like? I've been riding horses since I was three. I have my own and everything. I love going on roundup in the fall and spring and there are always new puppies and kittens to play with in the barn. It's hard to be bored when we always have things to do."

This very competent, very mature-for-her-age girl set a mug of cocoa in front of Sarah. "I mean, yeah, it might be cool to have a mall closer than Idaho Falls and something bigger than the one there. I'd also like to maybe be able to go to the beach sometime, you know? But I wouldn't trade it here for anything."

Sarah sipped at the delicious cocoa, trying to will away her sharp envy of the girl. She knew adults who weren't as comfortable with their world as this winsome young woman.

"Besides," Destry went on, "I have the *best* family. My dad is like the coolest dad *anywhere*. He's awesome, don't you think?"

Suddenly, she couldn't think about anything else but that moment when he had almost kissed her, right here at the kitchen table. "Yes. Awesome," she murmured, blaming the sudden heat of her cheeks on the steam from the cocoa.

Destry stirred her own mug of cocoa before sliding it onto the table and sitting down across from Sarah. "When I was a little kid, I used to be kind of sad about not having a mom like my friends did. I mean, I had Aunt Caidy and she was great and loved me and took care of me and stuff, but, you know, sometimes you still kind of feel like something's missing, right?"

Sympathy washed over her for this charming girl with the green eyes, freckles and huge capacity for love. "Yes. I completely understand," she said. "My parents divorced when I was small. I never really knew my father other than the occasional weekend."

"I didn't even have that. My mom just took off and then she died. We didn't know that until a while ago. I thought she just didn't want me and left."

"Oh, honey. I'm sure that's not true."

"My aunt Caidy thinks she would have come back eventually if she hadn't died. Who knows?" She sipped at her hot cocoa. "I don't think she was a very nice person. I can tell my aunt Caidy didn't like her. My dad doesn't talk about her at all."

Had Ridge's heart been broken by his ex-wife? she wondered. It wasn't a question she could ask the man's daughter.

"I hope I'm not like her," Destry said, for the first time showing a glimmer of insecurity that broke Sarah's heart.

"There's something else we have in common," she said quietly. "My father wasn't very nice, either. It's taken me a long time to see this, but I'm slowly coming to realize I can't let his decisions and weaknesses define me."

The truth resonated through her. Whatever her father or Joe might have done, none of it was her fault. She knew it, but she was no more eager to share her background or her suspicions with Ridge than she had been.

Destry sipped at her cocoa, swishing a mouthful around in her mouth as if she were testing fine wine.

"Do you want to know something funny? I used to feel really awful sometimes about her leaving, like, I don't know, I wasn't good enough for her to love me enough to stay or something."

Again, her heart was pierced by both the admission

and Destry's willingness to share it. "Oh, honey. You know that's not true, right?"

"Yeah. I do. Her leaving was about her, not me. And I know I could have had things a whole lot worse. Gabi lived with her mom for ten years, and it was a *nightmare.* She's a lot better off since her mom left her with Becca and Uncle Trace. And if she hadn't, Gabi wouldn't be my best friend and part of our family now."

"That's a good way to look at it."

"And I'm lucky, really. I might not have had a mom, but I've always had my dad and Aunt Caidy, which is more than a lot of kids."

She smiled, already crazy about Ridge's daughter. "You're an amazing young woman, Destry. Your family members are the ones who are lucky to have *you.*"

Destry grinned. "I guess we're one big, lucky, happy family then, aren't we?"

They were, while Sarah would be returning to her mostly solitary life. She tried not to let that depress her.

"Thanks again for your help today," Destry said. "I never would have been able to finish by Christmas. I can see why you're a teacher. You're really good at it."

"That's the best compliment I've had in a long time. Thank you."

Destry glanced at the clock. "I think the bread sticks have risen enough. Should I put them in or wait for Dad?"

"You would know that better than I do."

"I think I'll throw them in," she decided. "He'll probably come in the minute I pull them out of the oven. Somehow he always seems to know when dinner's ready."

Sure enough, the timer on the oven had only two minutes to go when the back door opened.

Destry giggled. "See? Told you."

A few moments later, Ridge entered the kitchen in stocking feet, bringing the scent of cold with him. His cheeks were rosy and wind-chapped, and she wanted to wrap him in that knitted blanket his daughter made for him and tuck him in by the fire.

"Man, are those bread sticks I smell?"

Destry nodded. "Yep. They're just about done. You've got perfect timing, as usual."

"You truly are the best daughter in the world."

He leaned in and kissed her cheek, and she shrieked. "Ack! You're like a block of ice! Even your eyelashes are frozen!"

"It's shaping up to be a bitter storm out there." He crossed to the sink and turned on the warm water to wash his hands.

"Were you able to get the heater working on the tractor?" Sarah asked him.

"It's not a hundred percent, but at least it's not blowing cold air. How's the arm?"

"It's actually feeling better."

"And the head?"

"Same story. I really think I would be fine on my own."

"Sorry, but I'm afraid we're not going anywhere this evening unless I hitch up a sleigh or drive you in on a snowmobile, neither of which would be very pleasant with that wind and blowing snow."

"Sleepover!" Destry exclaimed. "After dinner, we can roast marshmallows on the fire and have popcorn and watch a Christmas movie in our pajamas."

That idea actually sounded quite appealing while the storm howled and moaned around them. She had to admit, Destry's presence at the ranch left her feeling much less trapped.

"You Bowmans are nothing if not persistent," she said with a laugh.

Ridge smiled at her, and she was happy to see his cold-flushed cheeks already beginning to fade back to their normal tanned shade.

He really was extraordinarily good-looking, with those long eyelashes and the grooves beside his cheeks that she would never dare call dimples.

She found herself fascinated with that firm jawline, the mobile mouth. When she lifted her gaze to his, she found him watching her with an expression she could only call *hungry*. She shivered and looked away.

"Dinner is just about ready, but you still have time to take a shower and warm up the rest of the way." His daughter sounded like a little bustling mother hen, which made Sarah smile.

"I just might do that. Thanks, darlin'." He kissed Destry on the top of her head, gave Sarah a smile and headed out of the kitchen, leaving her head filled with all kinds of inappropriate images. Steamy water. Bare skin. Hard muscles. She took a hurried sip of her hot chocolate, which did absolutely nothing to cool her suddenly over-active imagination.

He couldn't remember an evening he had enjoyed more.

First they had the delicious slow-cooker stew along with hot, crusty bread sticks dripping with parmesan cheese. Dessert was ice cream and a few of the leftover goodies from the wedding.

While the storm howled like a kid having a tantrum, hurling snow at the windows and generally being a whiny, annoying pain in the ass, he and Destry and Sarah—and Ben Caldwell's funny little dog—sat in the cozy family room of River Bow with a fire flickering merrily away in the woodstove, watching Des's favorite Christmas movie, *Elf.*

He had always been partial to *Miracle on 34th Street* or *It's a Wonderful Life* himself—or Ralphie's BB gun travails in *A Christmas Story,* when he was in the mood for a good laugh. But Destry insisted that only *Elf* would do, even though she had watched the movie already at least three times that holiday season.

He didn't care. Right now, he was just happy to be out of the cold with a bowl of popcorn and a couple of pretty females to enjoy the movie with. He settled in to watch the silly but sweet fish-out-of-water movie about an overgrown elf trying to bring a little Christmas spirit to his grinch of a father amid the hustle-bustle of New York City. As always, he had to smile at the way Destry repeated all her favorite lines and laughed in all the same places.

He did his best, but he also couldn't seem to stop sneaking little looks at Sarah all evening. She sat beside his daughter on the sofa, her casted arm propped up on a pillow. When she smiled at the movie, he felt as if a warm sunbeam had just shot right through the window to rest on his shoulders.

He was aware of a sneaky, unexpected feeling of contentment. Winter nights were made for moments like this—the cozy, warm peace of being safe and dry and comfortable while the elements howled and raged outside.

He was one hell of a lucky man.

Their guest fell asleep about two-thirds through the movie, her head back against the sofa cushions and her mouth open just a bit. Poor thing. He wondered if she had had a chance to nap while he had been outside shoveling snow and preparing for the next onslaught. He doubted it. Judging by their animated conversation at dinnertime, Des probably yakked her ears off all day.

The two of them seemed to get along well. Maybe it was the educator in Sarah, but she treated Destry with respect, and his daughter seemed to thrive at the genuine interest she showed.

He would have to remember to thank her for temporarily helping to fill the gap left when Caidy got married. He had a feeling his daughter would miss her aunt—really, her surrogate mother—more than she wanted to admit.

It wasn't as if Caidy was going far, he reminded himself. She and Ben had a house just a few miles away with Ben's two children from his previous marriage and he expected Des would spend as much time there as she did here.

His sister loved his daughter deeply and would always be part of their lives, but Ridge knew this new phase of life for Caidy would be difficult for his daughter.

At least with the distraction of Sarah's company, Destry might be able to make it through the holidays with minimal emotional trauma—until their guest also left the River Bow and took her sweet smile back home to San Diego, anyway.

He didn't want to think about that tonight, especially

when the idea of her leaving left him with a hollow ache in his gut he had no business entertaining.

The closing credits to the movie started to play, and Destry sat up and stretched her arms above her head.

"I just love that one, don't you?" Destry asked the room in general.

Ridge pressed a finger to his lips and pointed to their guest, curled up beside her with her eyes closed.

"Oops," Des whispered with a wince. "Sorry. I didn't know she was asleep."

"She's had a couple of long days," he murmured. "This all has to be pretty unsettling for her, finding herself injured among strangers."

Destry looked thoughtful as she picked up the empty popcorn bowls and drink glasses and carried them into the kitchen. He followed after her.

"I really like her, Dad. She's super nice. We had a lot of fun today while you were out shoveling."

"Thanks again for fixing dinner. It was nice not to have to think of something to make."

"Sarah did the stew. I only made the bread sticks to go with it."

"Either way. Thanks." He glanced at the clock in the kitchen. "Wow, I didn't realize it was so late. You need to head to bed, too."

She made a face. "It's only ten-thirty, and I don't have school tomorrow."

"No, but I'll probably need your help clearing the sidewalk here and maybe at the Turners and Hansens," he said, naming the older neighbors on either side of the ranch who had trouble taking care of their own walks. Destry was a whiz with a snow shovel and she usually enjoyed it.

"Okay," she said promptly. "Hey, since it's Christmas Eve tomorrow, could we go for a sleigh ride later in the day, if the snow clears?"

"We already took all your girlfriends last weekend. You really want another one?"

"Just us and Sarah. She would like it, don't you think?"

He pictured her out in the sleigh with her nose pink from the cold and her eyes sparkling. "We might be able to arrange that. I'll see what condition the sleigh is in."

Usually when he took Destry and her friends, he used a wheeled hay wagon on plowed roads. It held more bodies and was easier on the horses. He hadn't used the smaller sleigh with runners in a few years. She would probably love it.

"Yay. Thanks!" She padded over to him in her silly little fluffy Rudolph slippers and hugged him.

At almost twelve, she was growing up so much, becoming a young lady right in front of his eyes. Before he knew it, she would be in high school, and all the boys would start flocking around her like cattle around the hay truck.

"Should I wake Sarah?" she asked.

"She looks pretty comfortable there by the fire. Let her sleep. I'm going to throw on my gear to take one last look around the ranch for the night to make sure everything is tight and secure in this wind. I'll wake her when I come back inside."

"Okay. Good night, Dad."

She started for the stairs with Tripod in her arms. Seeing her right about where Sarah had landed reminded him of something.

"Hey, I keep meaning to ask you. How would you

feel if Sarah spent the holidays with us? She doesn't have anybody else, and I feel bad thinking about her spending Christmas alone in the hotel, especially with a broken arm."

Destry smiled. "I think it would be great. I like her a lot. She's really nice."

He liked her, too. Perhaps a little too much.

"I'm trying to convince her, but she seems to think she'll impose. Maybe you can help me try to persuade her we have tons of space and would love the company. For most of the holidays, it would just be the three of us—at least until dinner at Taft's place on Christmas Day, and I know Laura won't mind setting out another plate."

"I'll try to convince her. It would be really fun to have her stay and I know *I* wouldn't want to be alone at Christmas."

"Whoever would you talk to, if you were by yourself?" he teased.

"Ha-ha." She made a face. "Good night, Dad. Love you."

"Love you right back."

He watched her pad all the way up the stairs in her silly festive slippers before he headed back to the mudroom for his winter gear again.

What he thought would be a quick fifteen-minute trip outside to make sure all hatches were battened down turned into an hour when he had to scramble to nail a couple of boards over a barn window that had shattered from a falling tree branch.

The welcome warmth of the house and the lingering scent of the apple-wood fire and their movie popcorn greeted him when he walked back inside, his bones aching from the cold and the twenty-hour day.

He loved the River Bow and had never wanted to be anything but a rancher like his father, but these sorts of days were long and hard—and, unfortunately, far from unusual.

He couldn't complain. He was doing exactly what he wanted with his life, something few people could claim. He was damn proud of what he had accomplished with the River Bow in the past twelve years. The ranch had always been prosperous—a rare feat in the transitory agricultural economy—but his father had been traditional, even a little staid, in his practices.

Through a few innovative changes, Ridge had managed to double the size of the herd while tripling the profit.

For all intents and purposes, the ranch was his. His brothers and Caidy loved the River Bow, but none of them was much interested in running it. Before she met Ben the year before and started taking online classes to become a veterinary tech, Caidy had trained horses and dogs and helped out where she was needed, but it had never been her passion.

He bore all responsibility for success or failure—and that was exactly how he liked it, even if it meant long, tough days like this one.

Yawning, he walked into the family room and found Sarah still sleeping there, though at some point in the past hour she had stretched out on the sofa and pulled a blanket over herself.

He gazed at her, lovely and serene in the flickering firelight through the woodstove glass and the multicolored glow from the little Christmas tree Caidy put up in this room.

For one crazy moment, he was overwhelmed with an odd feeling of *rightness* as he looked at her, as if she belonged exactly here.

Whoa. Slow down, he thought, more than a little disturbed at the direction of his thoughts. There was nothing *right* about Sarah Whitmore being on the River Bow. She didn't belong here, any more than Melinda had. She was a guest for only a few days, that was all, and he needed to remember that.

Her presence here was transient, just someone who would be drifting out of their lives as soon as she was up to it.

Yeah, he was fiercely attracted to her. Every time he looked at her, he had a funny little ache in his gut, the same feeling he had whenever he looked at a piece of his mom's art that particularly moved him.

He hadn't been looking for it and he didn't fully understand how he could be so quickly and completely drawn to a woman he still didn't know well. But there it was. He had it bad for her, and each moment they spent together only ratcheted up his aching hunger.

She wasn't for him, he reminded himself again. He needed to keep that clear in his head, no matter what kind of nonsense his gut—and other parts—tried to persuade him about.

With that in mind, he moved closer to the sofa. He hated to disturb her, but she would be far more comfortable in a bed where she could position that arm correctly.

"Sarah. Wake up."

Her eyelids flickered at his soft words, but she gave a delicate little sniff and closed them again. He was seriously tempted to lift her up and carry her to the bedroom like he used to do with Destry when she was small, but he had a feeling that wouldn't earn him any points with his houseguest.

"Sarah," he tried again. "It's late. Come on, wake up. Just for a minute. I'm sure it's cozy in here, but that fire's going to burn out soon and you'll be freezing. I promise you'll be better off in a bed."

"Tired," she muttered, her eyes still stubbornly closed.

He smiled at how very much she sound like Destry just now. Not knowing what else to do, he crouched down on a level with her. "Come on. Wake up. Let's get you to bed."

Unable to resist the beckoning appeal of that silky skin, he touched her cheek lightly with the back of his fingers. Her lashes fluttered once then twice and finally those blue-gray eyes opened.

She gazed at him, sleepy and disoriented. He knew the instant she recognized him. Her lips parted slightly, as if on a breath, and her eyes softened.

"Ridge. Hi." She spoke the words with a sweetness and welcome that stunned him, and for an instant, his emotions soared with such happiness he just wanted to crouch here beside the sofa and soak it in.

The impulse left him startled, even a little bit shaky.

"What time is it?" she asked, her voice a sexy rasp that shivered down his spine as if she'd trailed her fingertips there.

"Heading toward midnight," he answered, his own voice gruff. "Des went to bed more than an hour ago."

She sat up and rubbed at her neck. "Oh! I guess that means I missed the end of the movie."

"Yeah. I wouldn't worry about that at all. Destry will probably watch it all over again with you tomorrow if you want to catch the part you missed. She won't mind a bit, trust me."

She laughed a little and stretched out the arm not in a cast over her head. He had a tough time reminding himself to breathe.

"Come on. I'll take you to bed. Er, *help* you to bed."

He stumbled over the slip, hoping she didn't notice. Her sudden soft, very attractive blush indicated otherwise.

"You don't have to," she assured him. "I'm quite certain I can find my way the twenty feet to your sister's bedroom."

He managed a smile, when what he really wanted to do was press her back against those sofa cushions.

"Humor me. I just want to make sure you're not too wobbly, with that concussion."

She sighed and stood up. "Okay, fine. You can babysit me all the way to the bedroom, if that will make you feel better."

Yeah, he knew exactly what would make him feel better—and a bedroom was definitely involved.

He ground his back teeth, trying his best to force those all-too-appealing images out of his head, and followed her down the hall.

"You look cold," she said. "Have you been outside again in that weather?"

Okay. Good. Something safe to discuss. The intense blizzard was a great topic of conversation guaranteed to cool down his feverish thoughts. "Yeah. I went out to give things one last check before heading to bed myself. It was a good thing I did. A tree limb had knocked out a window in the barn. It took me a few minutes to patch over it."

"It's still snowing?" she asked, incredulity in her tone.

"I'm afraid so," he answered. "We're probably up to two feet by now. I sure do hope people had their Christmas shopping done already because I think most of Pine Gulch will be socked in for the next few days."

He opened her door. "Do you need anything? A glass of water? Midnight snack? More painkillers?"

"I should be fine, especially since your brother brought my clothes."

"Good. That's good." Her skin had to be the softest he'd ever seen on a woman, all creamy hollows and curves that begged for a man's mouth to explore....

"Um, good night, I guess," she said, her voice throaty again.

"Good night."

He gazed down at her, all sleepy, warm woman, and that sultry connection tugged between them.

He angled his head down without really even being aware of it just as she tilted her face up in an invitation he couldn't refuse.

Just one kiss, he told himself, only an experiment to discover if she could possibly taste as delicious as she looked.

His mouth brushed hers once, twice, tasting chocolate and buttery popcorn and Sarah. She didn't move for a long moment, and he was suddenly afraid he'd forgotten how to do this, but then she gave a tiny, sexy little sound and kissed him back.

She couldn't quite wrap her head around the idea that she was really here, kissing Ridge Bowman.

His skin was cool against hers—no wonder, since he had spent most of the day out in the harsh elements, poor man. She wanted to share her warmth with him, to tuck him against her until he absorbed some of her heat.

Any trace of sleepiness had long since disappeared, lost in the sheer wonder of the moment.

She was quite certain she had never been kissed like this, as if he couldn't get enough, as if he had spent a lifetime preparing for the moment their mouths would finally meet.

She wanted to savor every instant, every taste.

"I've been thinking about kissing you all day," he said, the gruff words vibrating through to her core.

"Have you?" she managed. It was a very good thing his arms around her were tough as steel or she probably would have dissolved to the floor in a quivering pile of hormones.

Even as passion flared between them, hot and bright, the tiny corner of her mind that could still string together a coherent thought was touched by the care he took not to jostle her broken arm.

"You're just about the sweetest thing I've ever seen. I can't get you out of my head. Crazy, isn't it?"

"Oh, yes." She didn't know if her breathy response was an agreement or simply a plea that he kiss her again just like that, right there at the corner of her mouth, that he wrap all those hard muscles around her and never let go....

He must have instinctively understood. They kissed for a long time, there in his cozy family room with the little Christmas tree glowing merrily in the corner. This felt so good, so right, she didn't ever want to stop.

Eventually, though, reality began to seep through the

wonder of Ridge's arms. This wasn't real. It was as fragile and insubstantial as silvery tinsel. Yes, he might be
attracted to her right now, but that couldn't possibly last
when he found out about her family.

Letting this continue was vastly unfair to him until
she could find the courage to admit the truth. They stood
on either side of a vast, unbreachable gulf…and she was
too much of a coward to even point it out to him.

Despising herself, she gathered the last ounce of
strength she had and eased away from him. "I… It's
late. We should probably both get some sleep."

For just a moment he froze, his expression still fierce
and hungry, then he drew in a breath, his features closing as if he had slammed a door.

"Yeah. It's been a long day."

His voice was stiffly polite, and she gave an inward
cringe, aware he thought she was rejecting him and
hadn't wanted him to kiss her.

How could she tell him otherwise without telling him
everything else?

She couldn't tell him she had never wanted anything
in her life so much as she had wanted to stand here in
the warm, cozy hallway and continue kissing this hard
rancher whose slow smile turned her insides to soft,
gooey taffy and who treated his daughter with such
kindness.

If she said any of that, he would ask why she had
stopped things—and she would have to tell him.

"Get some rest," he said. "I'll try not to wake you
when I head out early in the morning. I'll leave a note reminding Destry to keep things down in the kitchen, too."

"Thank you," she answered, not knowing what else
to say.

He seemed like a remote, distant stranger now, instead of the intense, passionate man who had kissed her as if he couldn't get enough.

She slipped into his sister's bedroom and closed the door carefully behind her. She waited, heart pounding, for him to walk away. It was another full moment before she heard his footsteps finally recede down the hall.

So he kissed her, Ridge thought as he banked the fire in the woodstove, then did the same in the great room before double-checking the locks and security system.

She was a lovely, unattached woman. He was a healthy male who hadn't been with a woman in entirely too long. Sharing a passionate kiss with her wasn't the end of the world, for crying out loud.

He was taking this rejection harder than he should. He had every reason to be decent about it. Sarah was a guest in his house. Beyond that, she was giving his family a gift of inexpressible worth. He could be polite, friendly, even warm to her, despite his disappointment and, okay, pissed-off attitude.

She hadn't asked him to kiss her. He had taken the initiative all on his own. While she had certainly kissed him back with undeniable enthusiasm—he hadn't been without a woman that long that he didn't recognize a genuine response when it licked his tongue—he still had no business being upset when she erected barriers between them again.

While his bruised ego would like to help her pack up her suitcase and drive her back to the Cold Creek Inn for Christmas, he knew he couldn't do that. He was a big boy. He could handle a little rejection.

He would rather have a little awkwardness between

them than the buckets of guilt he would have to carry around, thinking about her spending the holidays by herself in a hotel room simply because he had his boxers in a twist.

The last thing he did to shut the house down for the night was flip the switch to turn off all the Christmas lights.

He tried not to notice how the house seemed instantly colder—or how that chill suddenly matched his mood.

Chapter Nine

"I've never seen so much snow," Sarah exclaimed on Christmas Eve morning. It created a vast white sea—wave after wave, engulfing fence lines, shrubs, anything in its path. Across the way, snow had piled clear to the eaves of an outbuilding.

"The snowdrifts make it look a lot worse than it is," Destry said, with far more experience than an eleven-year-old girl ought to have.

"Do you think your father is okay out there?"

Destry looked surprised at the question, as if it had never occurred to her before. "Sure. Why wouldn't he be?"

Sarah could think of a dozen reasons. Frostbite. A fall from the tractor. A sudden howling avalanche. She shivered, not wanting to think about any of them.

"You must not have blizzards in San Diego," Destry guessed.

Sarah gave a rough laugh. "No. It's never snowed there in my memory, and I've been there since I was just a little girl. I think I read once it's snowed like five times in a hundred-fifty years. If we get more than a half inch of rain in twenty-four hours, people go into full-fledged panic mode."

"I love big storms like this, especially at Christmas," Destry said, expertly flipping a pancake just right.

The girl was amazing. Sarah knew fellow teachers who weren't as self-sufficient in the kitchen as this eleven-year-old girl.

"Why is that?" she asked.

"Seems like my dad takes a little more time to have fun, you know? We go sledding and ride the snowmobiles and have snowball fights. I like it when he can relax a little more."

Her expression grew a little sad. "Of course, this year won't be quite the same without Aunt Caidy. She and Ben won't be back until after New Year's Day."

"You'll still have a great Christmas. I'm sure of it." Sarah tried for a cheerful tone.

"Yeah. You're probably right. It's going to be different, that's all. We always spend Christmas Eve with just us and then we'll get together with the cousins for lunch tomorrow on Christmas. You'll like everybody, I promise. You already met Gabi and Trace, yesterday."

She nodded. "And Taft. He was one of the paramedics who took me to the hospital after my fall."

"Oh, yeah. Well, Becca and Laura are super nice and they have the *cutest* kids ever. Alex and Maya are Taft and Laura's two. Alex can be a little stinker but even when he drives everybody crazy, we can't help smiling at him. That's just the way he is. And Maya is so sweet.

She has Down syndrome, but that doesn't stop her chasing after Alex for a second."

"They sound adorable."

"They are. And then Trace and Becca had a baby earlier this year. William Frank, after my grandpa. Little Will. He has these big fat cheeks you just want to smooch all over. We all fight to hold him."

It sounded wonderful and warm and perfect. She fought down an aching wave of envy for this girl who knew exactly where she fit into the world, who was surrounded by people who cared about her.

Sarah didn't quite know how to break the news to Destry that she wouldn't be meeting any little fat-cheeked babies or cute little pesky cousins.

She had made up her mind sometime during the night that she would ask Ridge to dig out her rental car so she could return to the inn. The snow had stopped during the night and now the sun was shining. Though the snow seemed impenetrable, she imagined the plows would have a path cleared to town. If she drove slowly, she should be able to make it.

She would just have to be insistent, and if that failed, maybe she could find a taxi or something. At this point, she was even willing to walk.

She had practiced a dozen different arguments through the long, sleepless night.

While she didn't *really* want to leave this warm, comfortable house, she knew it would be for the best.

Yes, she felt an odd sense of belonging here at the River Bow, but she knew it was only an illusion. She could make believe otherwise but that didn't change the cold, hard reality. She was an interloper at the Bowmans' family Christmas and if they knew the truth about her background, none of them would want her anywhere near their adorable children, their holiday traditions.

That was enough of a reason for her to want to leave. Throw in the inevitable awkwardness between her and Ridge she didn't see how to avoid and she had even more incentive to return to Pine Gulch.

"Here you go. Buttermilk pancakes with homemade chokecherry syrup." Destry slid the pancakes onto a serving platter and pulled a little glass pitcher full of ruby-red syrup out of the microwave.

"We pick the chokecherries every year along the river and Caidy and I make jam and syrup. I guess we'll probably do that at her new house now with Ava and Jack. Those are Ben's kids from his first marriage. They're awesome, too, but I didn't tell you about them since I knew they wouldn't be there. They went with Caidy and Ben on their honeymoon."

"They took his children on their honeymoon?"

"And Mrs. Michaels, their housekeeper. They went to Hawaii. Ben and Caidy didn't want to spend Christmas without the kids, so they all went together, then Mrs. Michaels is bringing Ava and Jack back here while Caidy and Ben go to another island. Kauai, I think. I don't know, I've never been to Hawaii. Have you?"

"I went in college with some girlfriends," she said. She and Nicki and a couple of other friends had spent four days crowded into a tiny hotel room on Waikiki. It had been crazy and chaotic—not to mention expensive!—but she had great memories of the trip.

"It's all beautiful," she said. "I'm sure they'll have a great time."

"I guess. Ava was excited to go shopping. But that's Ava."

The Bowmans had this big, wonderful family, filled with interesting personalities. Under other circumstances, she very much would have enjoyed the chance to spend time with them all.

Some things weren't meant to be.

She and Destry were finishing up their pancakes when they heard footsteps coming up the back stairs and the outside door to the mudroom opening.

"That's Dad. I'd better cook a couple more pancakes. He likes his hot."

Destry jumped up while Sarah fought the urge to press a hand to her trembling insides.

A moment later, he came in wearing a green long-sleeve T-shirt and a pair of faded jeans that hung low on lean hips. He must have hurried out without shaving since a day's dark growth shadowed his lower face and made him look appealingly shaggy and disreputable.

"Hey, Dad! I didn't think you'd be in until lunchtime. Are you done?"

He smiled at his daughter—and while the smile might have encompassed her, it wasn't quite as warm as it might have been the day before.

"No. I finished our place and figured that was a good point for a break. I came in for more coffee and to see if you're ready to suit up and help me dig out the neighbors."

"Sure!" she said, with an eagerness that Sarah found amazing in a young girl. "Do you want a pancake or two and some sausage first?"

"Do you even need to ask?" he countered.

Destry laughed and poured more pancake batter onto the still-sizzling griddle. Sarah could only imagine how much fuel it took to power all day long through a physical job like ranching.

"I almost forgot! Merry Christmas Eve," he said to his daughter.

She grinned as she flipped his pancakes. "That's just what I was going to say. I think I like Christmas Eve better than Christmas. I'm always so excited, all day long. Today we're going on a sleigh ride, right?"

"You're relentless, my dear. I haven't had time to look at the sleigh but I'm still going to see what I can do, I promise. *After* we clear snow."

"I know. Work hard, then you can play hard. You tell me that like every single day."

"So I should get to say it twice on Christmas Eve."

She snorted and scooped the pancakes onto a plate for him. "There you go."

He smiled at her with warmth and affection as she turned off the griddle.

"I need to go put on my long underwear," Destry said.

"You can finish your breakfast first. I'm not going to take off without you."

"I'm *stuffed*," she said. "I had, like, four pancakes and three pieces of sausage. I'm going to be lucky to *fit* in my long johns. Anyway, I want to get the work done so we can hurry to the fun part."

She took a long drink of her milk, wiped her mouth with her napkin then barreled out of the kitchen.

The moment she left, taking all her energy and sweetness with her, an awkward silence descended on Sarah and Ridge.

This was the first she had seen him since that stunning kiss, and she didn't know what to say, where to look.

"Um, have you had a chance to dig out my rental car yet?"

He paused, mug of coffee halfway to his mouth. "Yeah. It's clear. You going somewhere?"

She realized she was fidgeting with her napkin and forced her hands to stop. "The sky is blue, with no more snow in sight for now. I imagine the roads should be clear by this afternoon. I can't see any reason not to return to the inn for the rest of my stay, can you?"

He set the mug down carefully, giving her a searching look. She could feel heat soaking her cheeks and really hoped she wasn't blushing.

"I thought we had you convinced to stay."

"It was a lovely offer and, believe me, I appreciate it. It's just…it's Christmas Eve. A time for families. I'm intruding, Ridge. You have been more than welcoming, but I can't help feeling like I don't belong in the middle of your Christmas celebrations. I had fully intended to spend the holidays on my own. I don't mind. I would be more comfortable back at the inn."

As far as lies went, that was a pretty big one. The idea of spending Christmas by herself, staring at the walls of a hotel room—no matter how warmly decorated—left her feeling bleak and achy from more than her lingering headache and broken arm.

The contrast between that image and the loud, chaotic, *wonderful* Christmas she imagined with the Bowman family was starkly vivid.

But what other choice did she have?

"Is this about what happened last night?" he asked after a long moment.

She flushed. "Are you accusing me of running away?"

"What else would you call it?" he countered.

She rested her hand on her lap, unable to meet his gaze. "Put yourself in my place, would you? Suddenly thrust into the lives of strangers by accident and your own stupidity. You and Destry already had Christmas plans before I showed up, and I've complicated everything. I think the best thing all around would be for me to return to town and leave you to your plans."

A muscle flexed in his jaw, and his chair squeaked a little as he shifted. "And the fact that we shared a pretty hot kiss just a few hours ago has absolutely nothing to do with your sudden eagerness to rush back to the inn?"

The memory of that *pretty hot kiss* flamed through her memory, fierce and bright as a flash fire. She had been up half the night reliving that kiss, his mouth hard and demanding, his fingers tracing patterns on her skin, those strong arms making her feel safe and cherished.

She didn't realize she was gazing at his mouth until his lips parted and he drew in a sharp breath. She jerked her gaze back to her hands.

"Okay, yes," she admitted. "I felt uncomfortable enough before, knowing I had intruded. Now things are even more…awkward."

He sighed heavily. "I'm sorry for that. I take full responsibility, Sarah. I shouldn't have kissed you. You're a guest in my home—and were injured here, to boot. I overstepped and I'm sorry. You shouldn't feel any awkwardness in the least—it's all on me."

"I didn't exactly push you away," she murmured.

Something bright as sunlight sparkling on snow flashed in his eyes. "No. You didn't."

That blasted color flared again, and she knew she must be as bright as one of the shiny glass ornaments on the tree. "I'm sure you agree it would be better for both of us if I returned to the inn."

"Maybe for you and me. But what about Destry?"

She frowned. "What *about* Destry?"

"This is her first Christmas without her aunt here. Her feelings are already tender. She likes you and considers you a friend. The two of you seemed to really hit it off, or am I imagining things?"

"No. She's...she's a wonderful young woman. You've done a great job as her father."

"I can't take much credit. Part of it was just the way she came and my family helped with the rest, but thank you. Our first Christmas without Caidy here is going to hit her hard. If you take off, too, who knows? She might feel abandoned all over again, poor thing. I'm sure you don't want that."

She narrowed her gaze. "You do *not* fight fair, Ridge Bowman."

He grinned suddenly and unexpectedly, looking years younger. "Whoever told you I did? Not my brothers, I'm sure."

She sighed, accepting defeat. While she was sure he was exaggerating his daughter's likely reaction to her leaving, she accepted that the girl missed her aunt in a hundred different little ways. The holidays might, indeed, be a bit of a struggle for her. If Sarah could help distract her for the next few days, how could she walk away?

"Fine. I'll stay a few more days, for Destry's sake. That's the only reason."

"Understood."

And no more kissing, she wanted to say, but she didn't have the courage.

Before she could change her mind or ask herself how she would endure even a few more hours with the two of them when they were already sneaking into her heart, Destry returned to the kitchen, bundled in snow pants, parka, hat, scarf and thick gloves.

"Okay. I'm ready," she declared. "Let's do this quick, before I have to go to the bathroom or something."

"Whew. Good thing I just finished my breakfast since apparently we're on the clock." Ridge set aside his napkin and slid his chair back.

"Will you be okay in here by yourself?" he asked Sarah. "We shouldn't be longer than an hour or so, since I did most of the hard stuff yesterday."

"Sure. I've got Tri to keep me company."

The dog yipped at his name, and Destry and Ridge both smiled.

"Don't worry about breakfast cleanup. Tri and I will take care of it, won't we, boy?"

The dog gave her a *speak-for-yourself* kind of look, as if to indicate he wasn't budging from the warm patch of sunlight on the floor.

"Just leave it," Ridge said. "We'll clean it up when we get back."

She didn't answer, just pointedly picked up her plate and started to scrape it into the kitchen garbage can.

"I mean it, Sarah. Go put your feet up or something."

"You'd better hurry. Those driveways aren't going to shovel themselves."

He gave her a long look, shook his head and then threw on his coat. She heard their murmured voices in the mudroom for a minute then watched out the window as he helped Destry hop up into the cab of the big tractor before following her and closing the door.

* * *

It charmed her more than it should, father and daughter heading out into the cold to help their neighbors together. She loved seeing it.

She thought of the little she knew of her own father from those carefully orchestrated visits. She couldn't imagine two men more different than Ridge and Vasily.

First of all, her father wouldn't have lifted a finger to help a neighbor. Not unless he were trying to steal the tractor right out from under them. Second, even if, by some wild stretch of imagination, he did have a tiny helpful bone in his body, he wouldn't have bothered to include his daughter in his efforts.

He had always treated her and Josef differently. As a young girl, she had grieved that she couldn't be what her father wanted. As the years passed and she realized Vasily was training Joey to follow in his footsteps, she could only be grateful her father had always seen her as lacking.

She pushed away the grim memories as she wiped down the countertops with a rag and dish soap that smelled like warm, juicy pomegranates.

It was Christmas Eve. She still could grab her keys and return to the inn. It was the safest choice, to escape while she still had half a chance to keep her heart intact.

Now that she was alone here in this quiet kitchen with only the sound of the refrigerator humming and the logs creaking and settling around her, she could admit the truth.

She wanted to be here.

She had spent so may cheerless Christmases when her mother was alive, feeling obligated to be with Barbara instead of accepting one of the many invitations that had been extended to her by friends.

This would be her first real family Christmas. She didn't care if she was merely borrowing someone else's holiday traditions. Now that she had made the decision to stay—or rather, now that Ridge had applied a little emotional blackmail to convince her of it—she intended to put aside her misgivings and throw herself into enjoying herself.

She would worry about the cost later.

"Oooh. Something smells good," Destry exclaimed, drawing out the last word to two syllables, as soon as they walked inside the warm house.

He had to agree with her. Cinnamon and vanilla, two of his favorite scents, drifted through the house with sweet, enticing promise.

"Sarah must be baking," he said, unbuttoning his coat.

"Cookies. I bet it's cookies," Des said eagerly.

"You could be right," he said. He took off his hat and shrugged out of his big ranch coat. How had Sarah managed to bake cookies when she only had one working arm? Everything must have been doubly hard, from measuring ingredients to rolling out dough.

Some kind of jazzy Christmas music played from the stereo in the kitchen. Even a grouchy old Scrooge like him could appreciate the perfection of the moment—fresh powder outside and a warm, cozy house that smelled like heaven.

As he slid off his boots, he tried not to think about how eager he was to see her again. She hadn't left his thoughts for more than a minute or two all day.

That heated, intense, surprising kiss the night before had left him restless and achy for things he knew he couldn't have.

She was a transitory part of their lives, he reminded himself. He had managed to convince her to stay another night or two but he had a feeling that wouldn't last long. No matter how he protested that she was very welcome to stay at the house, she seemed stuck on the idea that she was intruding on their family Christmas.

In a few days she would return to San Diego to her life and her students, leaving him to the hard reality of a lonely Idaho winter.

He told himself the sudden ache in his gut was only a pang of hunger that would be quickly dealt with by a cookie or two.

Destry beat him out of her winter gear and hurried into the kitchen. When he followed, he found the two of them with their heads together at the kitchen island, his daughter and the woman who was becoming entirely too important to him.

She flashed a tentative smile at him, looking sweetly uncertain. The ache in his gut intensified.

Okay, maybe he would need three cookies to ease it.

"Hi. How did the plowing go?"

Destry answered for both of them. "We kicked some blizzard butt, didn't we, Dad?"

He forced a chuckle. "Winter cleanup feels like a never-ending job sometimes around here, but I think the work is done for now. What are we baking?"

"Snickerdoodles. I make them with my students every year and I had a sudden craving. I hope you don't mind."

He had plenty of cravings of his own, suddenly. To

whirl her into his arms. To kiss the smudge of flour off her cheek. To press his lips to that soft, warm mouth....

"No," he murmured, his voice a little ragged. "I don't mind at all."

"Can I have one?" Destry asked.

"Of course," Sarah answered with a smile. She handed one to his daughter and then picked one up for him, too.

"Oh, wow. That's really good," Destry exclaimed.

"Will you help me finish baking them?" she asked his daughter. "I'm afraid I mixed up far more dough than the three of us can eat. We might need to freeze some."

"We can take some cookies tomorrow when we head to Taft's place for Christmas dinner," he suggested.

"Okay. There should be plenty. I'm used to cooking for twenty-four children and their families, I'm afraid."

"Hey," Destry exclaimed. "Maybe we could go take some to the Halls' house. I bet they're feeling kind of sad this year without Jason, don't you think, Dad?"

He smiled, touched at Destry's kindness. Caidy had done a good job of helping her think about others.

"Our neighbors' only son is finishing his residency in Utah," he explained. "His wife is having a baby in a few weeks and they can't travel, and the Halls have health issues and can't travel easily, so they're waiting until after the baby to go visit. They've been a little blue about spending the holidays alone."

"We should definitely take them a plate of cookies then," she exclaimed. "It will cheer them up."

"Could we take some to that nice new family that moved into the Marcus house?"

"You know, we were so busy with the wedding this year we skipped our little gifts to the neighbors. These cookies would be great. How about we combine activities? We can take a sleigh ride and distribute cookies on our way."

Sarah and Destry both looked at him with shining eyes that made him feel about twenty feet tall.

"Oh, that would be perfect," Sarah exclaimed. "I love it."

"Dad, you think of the *best* ideas."

He grinned down at his daughter. "I do what I can."

"Can we go after dark so we can see the lights?"

"How about we leave just before twilight? A couple hours from now. Then we can come back and grill our steaks."

"Steaks?" Sarah asked.

"Another Bowman family tradition," he answered. "My dad always fired up the grill on Christmas Eve. Mom would cook a big turkey for Christmas dinner but we always had a steak dinner on Christmas Eve. I guess it was his way of celebrating another year of keeping his cattle operation in the black."

"My mouth is watering already," she said.

When she smiled at him like that, soft and approachable, his mouth watered, too—and not for a juicy cut of beef.

Chapter Ten

"Are you warm enough?"

Sarah wrenched her gaze from the pristine winter scene ahead of them long enough to glance across the seat of the sleigh at Ridge, holding the reins.

He gazed steadily at her and she blushed, for reasons she couldn't have explained. "Oh, yes. We have about five blankets on, don't we, Destry?"

His daughter sat between them on the wide padded seat. "Maybe not quite but I'm not cold at all."

Though there was plenty of room, Sarah wished she was sitting behind them in the second row of seats. She had suggested it, but Destry liked to take a turn with the reins and neither of the Bowmans wanted her to sit by herself in the backseat.

As it made more sense to share the blankets and crowd together for warmth, they all sat together. Ridge wore his big lined ranch coat and a Stetson. He looked like something out of a sexy aftershave commercial, and every time she looked at him, she could feel her skin prickle with awareness.

"What about you?" she asked. "You're not using the blankets. Are you warm enough over there?"

"I'm great," he answered with a slow grin that made her insides jump and whirl like her first-graders after a sugar rush. "If you want the truth, I can't imagine anywhere I would rather be right now."

She had to agree. The night was clear and cold, with a vast expanse of starry sky overhead and a sliver of moon. The previous day's storm would have seemed like a distant memory if not for the deep snow piled up on either side of the road.

The sleigh bells on the big, sturdy horse's harness jingled in the night, the only sound besides the hooves thudding on snow and the steady whir of the sleigh runners.

They—and the prosaically named horse, Bob— seemed to be the only ones out on the cold night. Everyone else was probably hunkered in by the hearth having Christmas Eve dinner, singing carols, opening presents.

Like Ridge, she wouldn't have traded places with them for anything.

"This is magical," she said. "I keep thinking how my students would love to be in my place right now."

"Probably not *right now*," Destry pointed out. "Right now they're probably so eager for Santa to come, they don't want to be anywhere but their own houses. I know I always was that way when I was a little kid."

"You're still a little kid to some of us," Ridge said, earning a hard shoulder nudge from his daughter.

"Watch it or your driver will end up on the ground," he said with a laugh.

"Hey, don't call me a little kid. I'm almost twelve!"

"I know. Ancient. You'll be needing denture cream before you know it."

Sarah smiled at their interaction, charmed all over again by how close the two were. She almost didn't realize Ridge had directed the conversation to her.

"You mention your students all the time," he pointed out. "You must enjoy your work."

"I love being a teacher," she admitted. "The thing is, even when I'm not in the classroom, one part of my brain is always wondering how I can incorporate this experience or that piece of knowledge into my lesson plan. I wish you were closer. I would love to have you and Bob—and you, Destry, of course—come to class so we could have a lesson about horses. Or better still, a field trip to a working cattle ranch would be fantastic, wouldn't it? They would learn how you feed them, how much water they need, how ranching has changed over the time your family has owned the River Bow."

"That would be good. You know any cattle ranchers in San Diego?" he asked.

"No. I'm not sure there are any."

"There are. I can check with a couple of associations I belong to and see if I can find anybody in that area who might want to host a field trip."

"That would be wonderful. Thank you!"

A car approached from the other direction, and he turned his attention back to his driving, presenting her with that strong, handsome profile.

"You could bring them here," Destry said, her voice excited. "Wouldn't that be fun, Dad?"

"Sure," he drawled. "Might be a bit of a bus ride, though."

His words were a firm reminder of how much distance lay between their worlds, literally and figuratively. Some of her ebullient joy in the evening trickled out.

She forced herself to focus instead on how beautiful the Christmas lights looked, glowing through thick blankets of snow.

"I love how so many of your neighbors decorate their houses for the holidays."

"We're a pretty festive community, that's true," he answered. "Des, how many more cookie plates are back there?"

She looked behind him on the second row of seats. "One more. I was thinking we could give it to Mrs. Thatcher."

The girl turned to Sarah. "She's always *so* nice to me. Last time I shoveled her walk, she tried to give me five dollars, even though I told her I wanted to do it for free. I wouldn't take her money, but guess what? She mailed me an online gift card for fifteen dollars. Isn't that funny?"

"Wonderful," she answered with a smile, touched at the warmth and friendliness here in Pine Gulch. She knew a few of her neighbors in the condo unit where she lived in San Diego but this sort of community spirit seemed completely alien to her.

Ridge drove a little farther before reining Bob to a stop. Destry grabbed the last plate of snickerdoodles and hopped down effortlessly. "Be right back," she said.

Without the buffer provided by his daughter, Sarah and Ridge lapsed into silence broken by the jingling of the reins and the wind moaning in the trees.

They both watched Destry ring the doorbell, and a

moment later an elegant-looking older woman with carefully groomed hair opened the door.

"She'll probably want us to come inside, too, I'm afraid," Ridge said. "Don't worry. I'll make some kind of excuse."

"I can't imagine being friends with all my neighbors," she said. "You must love living here."

Though he still sat a Destry-sized space away from her, she could feel the air between them move when he shrugged. "Most of the time, I guess. It's all I've really known."

"Really? You haven't gone anywhere else?"

"Oh, on and off for school, though I finished a lot of my classwork through distance education. I met Destry's mother when I was working at a ranch outside Livingston, Montana, and stayed there a year."

He tilted his head back and gazed up at the stars. She wondered what he was thinking about. Old loves? People he had known and lost? Other starry nights?

"I wouldn't have stayed that long," he said after a moment, "but things were tense with my parents after I got married. They never liked Melinda much. She was too much of a city girl, and they figured she wouldn't be happy on the ranch. Turns out they were exactly right."

"Oh," she said softly. "I'm sorry."

"Just a week before they died, we fought pretty bitterly on the phone and I…said things that haunt me to this day. They wanted us to spend the holidays here that year so they could have the chance to get to know Melinda better. I refused, said it was too late to make nice. If they couldn't embrace my marriage, they could all spend Christmas in hell, as far as I was concerned. Yeah, I was pretty much an ass."

He was silent, gazing up at those stars, and she fought the urge to tuck the blanket around him in an effort to warm those suddenly wintry features.

"I can't stand knowing they died with ugliness between us, thinking I hated them," he said, his voice low.

A hard, sharp ache pinched her chest—for his pain and also for her connection to it. She reached across the space between them to place a hand on his arm. She could feel those leashed muscles even through the heavy lining of his coat.

"I didn't know your parents, but I've met several of your family members. From everything I've learned about Margaret and Frank since I arrived in Pine Gulch, I have to believe they knew you loved them. They strike me as the sort of people who would have been quick to forgive. I'm sure things would have eased between you eventually."

He drew in a long breath and then exhaled it slowly. After a pause, he covered her gloved fingers with his. She couldn't even feel his skin against hers, but the connection seemed profoundly intimate anyway.

"You're right. I know you are. They probably would have tried harder to accept the situation once they found out a baby was on the way."

"They didn't know about Destry?"

"No. I should have told them, but I was too angry at their reaction to Melinda. I didn't want to hear them say that was another strike against my marriage, that we had married for the wrong reasons. I had been thinking I would come for the holidays and tell them, but, well, I was too angry after we fought, especially at my father. Destry was born six months after their deaths. I wish they could have had the chance to know her."

"I'm so sorry."

He gazed down at her, silhouetted against the vast starry sky, and something sweetly tender, bright and glossy as Christmas lilies, bloomed inside her.

She was falling in love with him.

The realization didn't tumble over her like an avalanche, hard and wild and terrifying. Instead, it whispered down like a single, soft, plump snowflake, gentle and pure, followed by another and then another.

She swallowed. Oh. This was certainly unexpected.

She couldn't think or breathe or move. Love. How on earth had *that* happened? She couldn't be in love with him. She had only just met the man.

Common sense told her she was crazy, but she couldn't argue with the fragile tenderness fluttering through her.

Her heart would be broken into tiny jagged pieces when she left Pine Gulch.

She thought she enjoyed her life in San Diego. Her students, dinners out with friends, kayaking in Mission Bay. But right now, on this cold Christmas Eve, the idea of returning to her life seemed bleak and disheartening.

"What's wrong?" he asked softly.

Everything. She swallowed hard again. "Why do you ask?"

"You looked, I don't know, almost *bereft* for a moment. Is it your arm? It's probably aching in this cold, isn't it?"

"A little," she said, seizing on the ready excuse.

"You pushed yourself too hard today. Somebody who's only a few days out from a broken arm shouldn't be making cookies and gift wrapping."

Gift wrapping was probably a stretch to describe the

clumsy job she did packaging the few little things she had managed to find in her luggage to give the two of them.

"It was a wonderful day, Ridge. Thank you for allowing me to be part of it."

"We're the ones who should be thanking you. Those are mighty fine snickerdoodles. I'm really glad I have a couple more to go home to. As soon as Des comes out from chatting with Mrs. Thatcher, we'll head back to the ranch. The spuds you and Destry threw in the oven ought to be just about ready, and it won't take me long to grill up some steaks. Then you can get some rest."

She didn't *want* to rest. In a few days' time she would be back amid the seashore and sunshine of Southern California, and this would all seem like a distant dream. She wanted to savor every moment now, while she could.

As if on cue, Destry opened the door and came out carrying an overflowing basket.

Beside her, Ridge chuckled. "That's Ruthanne for you. She's probably afraid Des and I are going to wither away and starve without Caidy. She doesn't know we have all the leftover wedding food, not to mention about three months' worth of meals my sister stored up in the freezer for us."

Destry's flashlight beam lit up the night as she climbed back into the sleigh. "She's the *nicest* lady. I gave her one plate of cookies and ended up with this huge basket. A loaf of bread, homemade blackberry jam, some of that fancy cheese you like from the dairy in town, Dad. She said she had been planning to run it to the ranch tonight to thank us for shoveling her out."

"Well, then, I'm glad we saved her a trip. She would have slid all over the place with that old sedan of hers."

After much tucking and shifting, Destry was once more snuggled beneath the blankets with Sarah. When she was settled, Ridge glanced down at both of them.

"Well, ladies, should we head back for some Christmas dinner before all the goodies Mrs. Thatcher gave us freeze out here in the cold?"

"I *am* kind of starving," Destry said. "But take the long way back, okay? I want to go past my friend Kurt's house. He texted a picture of this awesome snowman family he and his brothers made."

"Snowmen, coming up." Ridge clicked his tongue to the horse. "Gee, Bob."

With Ridge guiding at the reins, the horse turned a corner at the next street, bells jingling. Sarah snuggled under the blanket and vowed to enjoy every moment of this one magical night she would have with them.

This was turning into his best Christmas ever.

It was loads better than the year he turned seventeen, when his dad had given him the keys to an old Chevrolet Silverado pickup truck. Better, even, than the first Christmas after Destry was born, when he still thought he might have half a chance at salvaging his marriage.

Christmas had always been his parents' favorite season, particularly his mother's. She would decorate the ranch house to the hilt, with trees in every room, fresh-cut garlands dripping from the mantel and the staircases, candles in every window.

Christmas music would play through the house from a few weeks before Thanksgiving through New Year's Day, until none of them could bear to jingle one more damn bell.

After his parents were murdered, the holidays took on a bittersweet tone for each of them.

He thought Caidy might have been most affected—with reason. She had been a sixteen-year-old girl, the only one of them not out on her own. The night of the murders, she had been home with Margaret and Frank and had ended up huddling on the floor of the kitchen pantry where their mother had shoved her at the first sign of intruders, where she had been forced to listen to her mother's dying moments.

For a long time, all of them had pretended to be overflowing with Christmas spirit for Destry's sake.

This year, for the first time since that awful Christmas season, he could actually claim his excitement was genuine.

The evening had been filled with laughter and fun. After the sleigh ride, he and Destry had quickly taken care of Bob and the sleigh and then returned to the house to finish dinner preparations.

The steaks had taken almost no time to grill while the girls performed an impromptu Christmas carol concert at the piano, with Sarah pecking out notes with one hand and Destry singing along.

Now they sat in the dining room with the candles lit and more soft, jazzy Christmas music playing out of the speakers.

"That was a delicious steak," Sarah said to him now, that soft smile lighting up her delicate features. "I enjoyed every bite, though it was a little humiliating that Destry had to cut it up for me."

"Anytime," his daughter said with a grin.

The two of them had developed a fast friendship. All evening, they seemed to have laughed together just as much as Destry did with Gabi. It warmed him to see it, even as he admitted to a few reservations.

His natural paternal instinct was to protect his daughter from hurt, even as he accepted that she needed to navigate a few little bumps in the road along the way in order to become a strong, capable woman and know how to handle the inevitable stresses in life.

But he had already failed to pick a loving woman to be her mother. Because of his poor choice, she would always have that void where her mother should have been.

Like it or not, she had suffered another emotional bump with Caidy's marriage.

How would she deal with one more loss of a friendship, even a fresh one, when Sarah returned to San Diego?

How would he?

He listened to their chatter while he tried to process how she could have become so important to both of them in such a short time.

He thought of those tender moments on the sleigh, the connection that had shivered and seethed between them. He was beginning to care about her deeply—and the idea of it scared the hell out of him.

He hadn't been looking for this. If somebody had asked him, he would have said he was perfectly content with the way his life had been going, that he didn't need anybody.

His marriage to Melinda had been such a hot mess he had just about decided he wasn't good at that sort of thing. Better to just stay single, raise his daughter, build the ranch. Maybe someday, long into the future when Destry was in high school or something, he could start thinking about a relationship. Something safe and solid and comfortable.

Suddenly Sarah tumbled into his life with her warm eyes and sweet smile.

He had it bad. He couldn't be in the same room with her without wanting to kiss her, taste her, touch her.

He pushed away his plate. Spending this magical Christmas Eve with her had only reinforced how empty his world was the rest of the time.

"What now?" Destry asked. "We could watch *Elf* again. Sarah never saw the end."

He enjoyed the movie, but he didn't necessarily want to watch it for the second time in as many days. "How about my favorite? *It's a Wonderful Life*."

"I guess," Destry said. "I do like that one, too. I'll pop the popcorn."

"After you just had a steak dinner? How about we pass on the popcorn?"

"I'll pop some just in case we want some later," Destry said.

A short time later, they settled into the family room in roughly the same spots they had been for the previous movie, with him in his favorite recliner and the two of them snuggled in blankets on the sofa.

He would have liked to ask Destry to switch places with him but he didn't think either of them would appreciate the suggestion.

The movie was a long one—and, once again, Sarah fell asleep during the last half.

It was quite endearing to watch her try valiantly to stay awake, but finally her eyelids seemed to get heavier and heavier with each blink until she slumped to the side with her mouth open a little.

Destry noticed the same thing after a few minutes and grinned at him. "I guess she has a hard time staying awake in movies," she whispered.

"Looks like," he answered. Maybe she had also struggled to sleep after that stunning kiss they shared. It was probably small of him, but he hoped so.

This time, she woke up just as the little bell on the Christmas tree rang, heralding the angel Clarence earning his wings.

He was watching her more than the movie and enjoyed the sleepy way her eyes blinked open. "Oh," she exclaimed on a yawn, her voice thready with sleep. "I love that part."

The credits started to roll, and she rubbed at her eyes. "I must have dozed off."

"You did!" Destry said. "You tried really hard not to, but I guess you were just too tired."

"How much did I miss?"

"I don't remember. Dad? When did she fall asleep?"

He knew exactly when, right down to the moment in the scene. Would admitting that to her make her wonder just how closely he had been watching?

"Right about the time George Bailey sees how the old crumbling house would have been falling apart without him."

"And finds his beloved wife a lonely spinster," she murmured. As she said the words, color flared in her cheeks, and he wondered at it.

"Yep," Destry said. "That movie just makes me happy. Now I don't know which one is my favorite Christmas movie, *Elf* or *It's a Wonderful Life*. They're both so good."

"No reason you have to decide tonight. In fact, we're

heading for eleven. You should probably go to bed. Remember, Santa Claus can't come unless you're asleep."

She rolled her eyes. "Dad. I'm eleven and a half, remember?"

"So? You think he has different rules for smarty-pants girls who think they're almost teenagers?"

"You're such a dork," she said with a wry grin. Still, she hopped off the sofa. "But I am tired. I guess I should think about bed. Are we going to read the Christmas story first?"

"Why don't you get in your pajamas first, then we'll read in the great room by the fireplace and the big Christmas tree."

"Deal."

She hurried from the room with the same energy she brought to everything.

"We always read the story in Luke," he explained to Sarah when the two of them were alone. "It was kind of a tradition with my parents. You don't have to stay if you don't want to."

"You and Destry are trying to build your own traditions. I can go to bed if you would rather just read the story with your daughter."

"Not at all. You're more than welcome. Come in, and you can help me add a couple more logs to the fire."

Though he knew touching her probably wasn't a good idea, proper host etiquette and simple human courtesy demanded he reach out a hand to help her to her feet.

When she rose, she was only a few inches from him. He could feel the air currents swirl around them with each inhale and exhale.

She gazed up at him, and he thought he saw *something* there, something bright and tender.

"Sarah—" he began, but whatever he meant to say next caught somewhere in his throat, all tangled up in his overwhelming desire to kiss her.

She leaned toward him, her breasts brushing against his chest, lips slightly apart and the flutter of her heartbeat at the base of her neck.

She wouldn't push him away. Not this time.

Call it male arrogance, call it instinct. He didn't know how he knew, but he did.

He leaned down, just enough, but a half second before his mouth would have found hers, they heard footsteps hurrying down the hall.

He eased back again just as Destry raced into the room at full speed.

"All done," she said proudly. "That was the fastest change on record, right?"

"Painfully fast," he muttered. "I didn't even have time to build up the fire."

Sarah made a small sound in her throat that might have been amusement or dismay, he couldn't tell.

"I also need to grab my dad's Bible out of the china cabinet in the dining room."

"I'll find the Bible. I know where it is. I found it when I was helping Caidy look for a few things for the wedding. You two take care of the fire," Destry ordered.

"Yes, ma'am."

As far as he was concerned, they had been doing just that, and he would have liked a chance to get back to it. This was obviously not the moment, with his daughter running around. After a pause, he headed into the great room, where tree lights already glowed, sending a kaleidoscope of color throughout the room. She followed, settling onto the sofa there while he added a few new logs to the fire he had started earlier in the evening.

"Am I supposed to be helping with the fire, according to Destry's script?" she asked.

He laughed. "She tends to want things a certain way. I have no idea where she gets that."

"I can't imagine," she murmured.

He again wanted to sink down beside her on the sofa and leave Destry to sit by herself on the other sofa but he decided that would be entirely too selfish of him.

A moment later, his daughter walked in with her arms wrapped around the black leather Bible Ridge had watched his father read just about every morning of his life after chores.

"Here you go, Dad." She handed him the black King James Version that had Franklin Paul Bowman etched in gilt letters across the front.

He gazed down at it as a hundred memories flooded back to him. Going to Sunday school when he was a kid, his thick wavy hair tamed with copious amounts of gel, pinching the twins to be quiet as they tried to wrestle on the pew. Listening to his father talk about his reverence for the land and his relationship with God while they were out on the tractor.

At the forefront were those last bitter things he had hurled at his father just days before he died—that he was tired of Frank trying to run his life, damn sick and tired of being treated as if he didn't have the brains or the balls to figure things out on his own, that he couldn't respect a man who didn't see his own son was a grown man trying to live his own life.

He pushed that memory away, focusing instead on all those years of his childhood when his family would gather right here and read about babies and miracles and gifts from above.

He opened to the well-worn page in Luke, carefully highlighted in red pencil by his father's hand. He'd read from this Bible every Christmas since coming back to River Bow, but he'd never noticed the small note in the margin at one verse, in his father's handwriting, underlined three times.

"Fear not!" the note read. For some reason, the words seemed to jump off the page at him, as if his father were trying to tell him something.

He gazed at it for a long time, until Destry finally spoke.

"Dad? Aren't you going to read?"

"Um. Yeah. Sorry." He cleared his throat and began reading. "'And it came to pass…'"

When he looked up after reading the last highlighted verse, Destry's eyes were bright with happiness.

"I never get tired of hearing that," she declared.

Sarah's eyes were bright, too, but if he wasn't mistaken, they were shiny with emotion.

"That was lovely," she said, her voice soft. "I don't think I've ever heard the story read so beautifully."

That subtle connection seemed to shimmer around them like a shiny garland.

"I had a good example. My dad read the story as if he had been one of those shepherds suddenly shaken out of their normal world by a host of angels."

She smiled, and he was suddenly deeply grateful for her. If she hadn't been here, would he have found any sliver of Christmas spirit this year? Or would he have simply continued trudging through the motions to make sure his daughter enjoyed the holiday?

Destry gave one of her ear-popping yawns, big enough to show off her back molars.

"You need to be in bed, missy. And no sneaking down to see what Santa brought you before I have a chance to be there with you."

"I won't," she promised. She padded to him in her silly slippers and threw her arms around his neck. "I love you, Daddy. Merry Christmas."

He hugged her, a ridiculous lump in his throat. "Love you right back, ladybug."

She made a face at the name he had called her since she was a toddler. To his surprise, she went to Sarah next.

"Merry Christmas. I'm so glad you were here this year. You made everything more fun."

He saw Sarah's eyes widen with astonishment when Destry threw her arms around her neck. After a shocked moment, she hugged her back.

"I had a wonderful day," she said. "Good night. I'll see you in the morning. Merry Christmas."

When Destry headed up the log staircase to her room, he suddenly realized he was alone with his houseguest again.

"You're probably exhausted, too," he said.

"Not really. That nap sort of took the edge off. Right now I'm not tired at all."

"I've got to wait about an hour until I'm certain she's asleep before I play Santa Claus. Do you want to help?"

"Oh!" she exclaimed, looking intrigued. "That sounds fun."

"I have to admit to being selfish about this part of Christmas. The way things have always worked out in the past—and even this year, with all the craziness of her wedding, if you can believe that—Caidy has always done a lot of the holiday shopping for me. She even wraps most of the presents. She's good at it so I let her, but I always tell her I like to play St. Nick. I always like filling the stockings and setting everything out around the tree. Thank you for keeping me company."

"You're welcome."

"Can I get you something to drink?"

"I've been thinking all day about that delicious raspberry cocoa Destry made yesterday."

"You got it."

Cocoa actually sounded great to him, too. Perfect for a cold Christmas Eve. He quickly heated water and mixed in the gourmet cocoa packets Caidy had left behind—raspberry chocolate for Sarah, mint chocolate for himself. When the mix dissolved, he carried the mugs back to the great room, where he found her gazing at the Christmas-tree lights reflected in the front window.

This time he did sit beside her on the sofa, and she moved her feet a little to make room for him.

They sat in surprisingly companionable silence, especially given the currents that seemed to zing between them.

"These past few days you've had a taste of the Bowman Christmas traditions. What about the Whitmore Christmas traditions?"

She tensed at the question with the mug halfway to her mouth. "What about them?" she asked, her tone far more defensive than he might have expected.

"I'm curious. That's all. I've noticed you have a habit of not talking much about yourself. It's tough to get to know you when you don't share much."

"I told you my parents divorced when I was young,

and that I…didn't have much of a relationship with my father."

"Yes. I'm sorry for that."

"I could tell by the way you cherished your father's Bible this evening how much you miss him. Mine died only a few months ago, and I don't miss him at all. Does that make me a terrible person?"

"It makes you normal, Sarah. You didn't know the man. You can't grieve for someone simply because you happen to share his DNA."

She was quiet, her fingers picking at the edge of the soft fleece blanket she had tucked around her feet. "If I grieve for any loss," she finally said, her voice low, "it's the fantasy I had of a good, loving father who wanted the best for me. The kind of father you are to Destry."

Emotion rose in his throat again, both at the sweetly touching compliment she had just paid him and for everything she had missed in her childhood.

"What about your mother?" he pressed. "Did you have any traditions with her?"

"We went to church every Christmas Eve. I don't remember much besides that. I can tell you that I was never so stirred in a church service as I was tonight by the way you read the simple story."

She gazed at him, her eyes soft, and he felt something sparkle to life in his chest like someone had just plugged in a hundred Christmas trees.

He was falling hard for this lovely woman who treated his daughter with such kindness.

Fear not.

That little phrase written in his father's hand seemed to leap into his mind.

Fear not.

He was pretty sure this wasn't what his father meant—or the angels on that first Christmas night, for that matter—but he didn't care. It seemed perfect and right to fearlessly take her mug of cocoa and set it on the side table next to his own, to lean across the space between them, to lower his head, to taste that soft, sweet mouth that had tantalized him all day.

Chapter Eleven

She knew they shouldn't be doing this, but kissing Ridge Bowman was an irresistible joy and she couldn't seem to summon the strength to stop.

"All day long, I've been thinking about kissing you again."

She shivered at his low words against her mouth. Tenderness for this man—solid, steady, ranch-tough but achingly sweet—fluttered inside her like a tiny, fragile bird.

Her entire life, she had dreamed of a man like him. Someone she knew would cherish her—a man who would see and appreciate her strengths, who would love her despite her weaknesses.

How could she ever have imagined she would find him here—or that she would have to walk away before she really had the chance to savor this unexpected wonder?

She returned the kiss, pouring all the emotions she couldn't tell him into it. He smelled delicious—soap and some kind of outdoorsy aftershave—and tasted even better, of chocolate and mint.

Her casted arm seemed to get in the way, even though he took great care not to jostle it, and she fleetingly wished that she didn't have the bother of it.

As soon as she had the thought, she pushed it away. She never would have believed she could be grateful for breaking her arm. If she hadn't, though, she would have dropped off the painting and returned to San Diego to arrange delivery of the rest of the collection.

She never would have known Ridge or Destry other than as strangers she had once met. She never would have discovered how very appealing she found a man who cared deeply for his daughter and was trying to do right by her under hard circumstances.

She never would have guessed that first day she showed up at the doorstep that she would enjoy the most joy-filled Christmas of her life in company with a tough rancher and his irrepressible daughter.

Yes, leaving them was going to hurt—so badly she didn't know how she would bear it and was already bracing herself for the inevitable pain. But she wouldn't have missed this chance for anything, this rare and infinitely precious moment tangled around him while the tree lights gleamed and the fire crackled beside them.

They kissed for a long time—deep, lingering, intoxicating kisses that left her achy and restless for more.

Finally he drew away and rested his forehead against hers. "I can't believe I've only known you a few days.

You're perfect. The most wonderful woman I've ever met. I feel like I've been waiting for you my entire life. You fit perfectly into our lives, as if you've been at the River Bow forever."

The husky words pierced the soft, delicious haze surrounding her. She had a wild rush of joy that he was beginning to care for her, too, and then the reality crashed down as if the whole Christmas tree had toppled onto the two of them, shattering ornaments and lightbulbs and angels.

Oh. Oh, no. How could she have been so selfish? This wasn't all about her. She had been so wrapped up in thinking about how she would hurt when she left she hadn't given any thought to his feelings. What if he were coming to care for her, too? He would be even more angry when he found out the truth.

Heart aching with the words she couldn't say, she eased away, desperate for space between them.

The tenderness in his gaze raked her conscience with sharp talons. She was here—in his house, in his arms—under false pretenses. When he found out the truth, those kisses she considered sweetly magical would seem tawdry and wrong.

She was making everything worse by pushing her way into their lives, fooling them into beginning to care about her. If she had thought of the consequences, she never would have come here.

"Don't you think we should put the presents out now?" she said, hoping he didn't hear the note of desperation in her voice. "I imagine Destry's asleep by now."

He gazed at her for a long moment, a tiny frown between his brows. "Yeah. You're right," he finally said.

"I've got them all stored in a corner of the attic. Give me a minute to carry them down."

"Do you need my help?" she asked, grateful that her voice wasn't trembling as much as she feared.

"No. I've got it."

She nodded and curled her legs up beside her on the sofa. While she waited for him to return, she gazed into the fire and seriously considered leaving. Just packing her things right now at nearly midnight on Christmas Eve and driving away.

She couldn't do that to Destry. After the wonderful day they'd had today, the girl would be hurt at such an abrupt departure.

But how could she stay, when each moment with Ridge sent her tumbling further and further in love with him?

What a mess.

She pressed a hand to her stomach, wishing on all the Christmas stars in the sky that things could be different.

A moment later, Ridge came down the stairs carrying a huge plastic bin piled high with wrapped presents.

"Here we go," he said, setting the bin down by the tree. "I'll fill the stockings while you set the other presents under the tree."

All over the world, parents who celebrated Christmas were doing this same thing, she thought with a little amazement. Perhaps with only a gift or two, perhaps with grand expensive gestures.

Her part didn't take long, then she turned back to watch Ridge, more charmed than she wanted to admit as she watched him fill a stocking with oranges, candy, small wrapped packages.

"Did you wrap the presents yourself?" she asked him

as she looked at the artful pile of gifts under the massive tree.

"Some of them. I would guess Caidy bought and wrapped about half of them. I did the rest. I'm not sure how she found time to think about Destry's Christmas gifts leading up to the craziness of the wedding, but somehow she managed. She actually starts pretty early in the year and is usually done by Thanksgiving, so that probably helped."

"She sounds like an amazing person."

"She is. I think you'll like her, and I know she'll love you."

That guilt settled low in her stomach. She wouldn't have the chance to meet Caidy Bowman Caldwell. By the time his sister and her veterinarian husband returned from her honeymoon, Sarah would only be a memory to Ridge and his daughter—and not a very pleasant one.

"There. That should do it." He carried the stocking over to the mantel, where a heavy brass stocking holder was already in place, then he returned to the table where he had the little bits and pieces of leftover candy and began to fill two more.

Two. One for himself, she assumed, and one for her.

"You have a stocking for me?"

He looked up, surprised. "Of course."

He held it up and she saw it was a lovely hand-sewn stocking made from a shimmery burgundy material.

"Where did it come from?"

"The attic. I found it in a box of one of the old Christmas things while I was up there. That's what took me so long." He paused and studied her with an expression she couldn't decipher.

"It was my mom's. I figured she would be delighted to share with you."

His mother's. The woman who had created that work of stunning beauty over the mantel and the tender portrait of her daughter that vibrated with Margaret's love for Caidy. The parent who hadn't lived long enough to see her first grandchild—or all the children who had come after, adopted into the family or biological.

As she looked at those big, callused hands holding the delicate thing, thick emotions welled up in her throat and spilled over.

He immediately looked horrified. "Hey. Don't cry. I didn't mean to upset you. I just didn't want you to feel left out and have nothing on Christmas morning."

She let out a hitching little sob. "You've been so wonderful to me. I've never known such a happy Christmas. I mean that. Thank you for sharing your holiday with me, Ridge. I can't begin to tell you how much I have enjoyed every moment."

He gave a rough laugh. "That's funny. You look like your heart is broken or something."

It was cracking apart. Surely he could see the pieces lying there on the floor. "I just…don't deserve your kindness and generosity. I'm a stranger."

"Not anymore, Sarah. Can't you see that? You will always be welcome at the River Bow."

Oh, how she wished that were true. She should tell him everything, right now. The weight on her conscience was becoming more than she could bear.

How could she ruin his Christmas by bringing such dark ugliness into it? Just a few more days, she told herself. Then she would be honest with him for the first time.

She continued the lie by forcing a smile. "Thank you

for that, and for the stocking. It was remarkably kind of you. That's the reason for the tears—your kindness, and the fact that my arm is letting me know it's been a long day. I should probably turn in."

He gave her a searching look, but she forced her features into what she hoped appeared as calm composure.

At all costs, she had to keep the love and tenderness out of her expression. If he knew how much she was coming to care for him and his daughter, everything would be much worse.

"Good night. Merry Christmas."

"Merry Christmas." She smiled, drew in all her strength and kissed the corner of his mouth with feigned casualness, then slipped away before he could pull her into a deeper embrace.

Something was definitely eating her.

Ridge watched Sarah walk to her bedroom, each step measured and her head sagging as if her neck couldn't support the weight of whatever was bothering her.

He had no idea how to bridge the distance she seemed so determined to keep between them.

Maybe he needed to stop trying.

His feelings for her were growing, but that didn't automatically mean she felt the same thing. He closed his eyes. No. He had seen *something* in her gaze, something soft and tender and real, like the star on the very top of the Christmas tree, but then she pulled away before he could reach for it.

With a sigh, he hung the other two stockings then went about his routine of shutting down the house— banking the fire, turning off lights, making sure all the doors were locked.

He left both Christmas trees on, another Bowman family tradition.

"Santa's got to find his way here somehow, doesn't he?" Frank would always say with a wink, even when Ridge and the boys were into their late teens.

Perhaps that was the core of Sarah's misgivings. From the few things she had told him, his heart ached for what sounded like a painful childhood.

Of the two of them, he was far luckier. Yes, his parents had been taken from them all in a terribly tragic way. But at least he had known twenty-four happy Christmases with them—okay, twenty-three and then the one where he'd just been an ass.

Judging by what little she had said, and her astonished joy in everything they did that day, her childhood holidays must have been dry, cheerless affairs.

This year would be different for her, he vowed. Tomorrow he would do everything he could to give her the bright day full of hope and promise that she deserved.

He gave the tree one last look, ran a hand down his father's Bible still sitting on the side table, then headed for the solitary bed he had slept in for the past twelve years, wishing fiercely that things could be different.

Watching Destry Bowman on Christmas morning was a sheer delight, Sarah thought.

The girl was grateful for every gift she opened, from a collection of lip glosses her father confessed to picking out himself to a new eReader she had been wanting "for *ages,*" she declared dramatically.

If Destry could be this excited about Christmas at nearly twelve, Sarah could only imagine the girl's reaction a few years earlier.

She loved this glimpse into their lives, seeing the bond between father and daughter. Ridge was a great father—firm but loving.

He should have had more children, she thought, and fought down a pang of sympathy that his life had taken a very different road than he probably expected.

"Looks like there are only a few left," Destry said. From under the tree, she pulled out the big, beautifully wrapped box Sarah knew contained the gift the girl had made for her father.

"Hey, this one's for you," she said in mock surprise. "I wonder what it could be?"

Ridge chuckled. "I have a feeling you know the answer to that."

"Maybe. Well, open it already!"

Ridge looked down at the box. "The wrapping paper is so pretty. Whatever it is, somebody put a lot of time into wrapping it."

"It's from me, okay? Open it, would you?"

He laughed again, clearly enjoying teasing his impatient daughter. "Haven't you ever heard of anticipation? Savoring the journey instead of always rushing headlong to the destination? Maybe you should work on it sometime."

"I will," she promised. "Just not right now. I've been *dying* for you to open my present. You're going to *love* it."

Sarah found it touching, and another mark of excellent parenting on Ridge's—and his sister Caidy's—part that, as excited as Destry had been about opening her own gifts, she seemed even more thrilled to be giving her handmade, from-the-heart gift to her father.

"All right, all right," Ridge finally said. He took the

box on his lap and started carefully removing the wrappings. By the time he pulled off the last bit of wrapping, even *Sarah* was on the edge of her seat with anticipation.

She suddenly had no doubt that he would make love with the same deliberate, focused attention.

She blushed at the inappropriate thought, right here in the middle of a family Christmas. What was the matter with her? Her mind was entirely too unruly when it came to him. She pushed away the thought as he opened the lid to the box and pulled out the richly colored throw.

"Oh. This is beautiful, Des. Did somebody make it for you?"

"No! I made it, all by myself! Well, okay, Becca showed me the stitches and helped me work on it while I was there, and then Sarah helped me finish it. But I did most of it all on my own."

His tough features softened as he looked at his daughter. "Wow! This is amazing. It must have taken you hours!"

"A few," she admitted, quite humbly, since Sarah knew she had spent much more than a few on the project.

He pulled it out and laid it across his lap. "I can't believe you did this."

"I thought my fingers were going to fall off," she confessed, though her cheeks were pink, her eyes shining. She looked as if her father's reaction was everything she had imagined and more.

"Do you know what this is? The perfect thing for lying on the couch and sleeping while I'm pretending to watch a ball game."

"I know! That's just what I thought you could use it for."

He laughed and held out his arms. "Thank you. I *love*

it. It's beautiful, and it means so much more because you took the time to make it. Come here, ladybug."

She hugged him and the love between father and daughter touched a small, lonely part of her heart.

"Thanks for my great Christmas, too," Destry said. "It's all been perfect."

"What about those last few gifts?" Ridge asked.

"Oh, yeah," Destry said. She winked at her father in a not-so-subtle way and then pulled them from beneath the lowest limbs of the tree and carried them both over to Sarah.

She looked down at her name clearly marked on the outside, then back at the two of them.

"Oh. You didn't have to get me gifts," she exclaimed.

"Like you didn't need to give us gifts?" Ridge drawled.

"Mine weren't much," she said, though she could feel her face heat again. "I haven't exactly had a chance to go shopping since I've been here."

The first night she arrived in Pine Gulch, before she had come out to the ranch, she had wandered around the small downtown, peeking her head into a few gift shops. She had been very grateful for her few impulse purchases the night before when she was trying to think of what to give them.

For Ridge, she had given him the book on Pine Gulch history she had purchased on a whim. For Destry, she had a pair of finely wrought silver-and-turquoise hoop earrings and a bottle of scented lotion she had originally purchased for Nicki. She would find something else for her friend.

She opened Destry's gift first, and when she saw it,

her heart swelled. "Oh, honey. It's beautiful. When did you have time to make this?"

"I worked on it the last two nights in my room after I went to bed. You might not have all that many chances to wear scarves in San Diego but maybe once in a while."

She pulled out the colorful scarf, knitted out of soft yarns of variegated green and peach, touched beyond measure to think of the girl working late in her room to make a gift for an unexpected houseguest she just met.

"I'll make the chance," she promised. "And every time I wear it, I'll remember this wonderful Christmas with both of you."

She fastened it around her neck, looping it in half and pulling the ends through.

"Now the other one," Destry said, her eyes bright. "It's from both of us."

This one was rectangular and narrow, roughly eighteen by twenty-four inches. She pulled away a bit of wrapping paper and saw an edge of a black picture frame. Heart pounding, she pulled away the rest of the paper.

"Oh."

She couldn't breathe for a long moment and could feel tears burn her eyes. It was a lovely framed print of the River Bow, obviously painted from the perspective of the foothills above the ranch.

She could see the distinctive log house and the beautiful red barn, as well as the other landmark building she recognized, all painted in a summer scene with wildflowers in the foreground. The silvery bright Cold Creek wound around the edge of the scene, forming the distinctive bow the ranch was named for.

"Your mother painted this one, as well," she said softly. "I recognize her style."

Ridge nodded, shifting a little uncomfortably. "It's one of the few she had made into prints, so we have others of this same scene. I just thought you might like to have something to remember us."

Yes, it might be a print, but she didn't doubt it was also valuable, considering the increasing recognition of Margaret Bowman's rare talent in art circles.

She wanted to tell him she couldn't accept it, that it wouldn't be right. He would probably agree with her once she returned all those other paintings to the family. The words caught in her throat. She couldn't say that now. Refusing the gift would be churlish of her, especially when she very much wanted to keep it.

When she returned to San Diego, she would probably wonder if all of this had been a dream. The art print would be a tangible reminder to her of these amazing few days, to go with all the memories she knew would haunt her.

"Thank you," she murmured solemnly. "I will cherish it always."

Something in her tone seemed to disturb him. He gave her a careful look and tension shivered between them.

"I guess that's it, then," Destry said, beginning to gather up wrapping paper.

"For now. We've got more fun planned at Taft's this afternoon. That breakfast casserole Caidy froze for us should be just about ready to come out of the oven by now. I'll throw some waffles on the iron and then we need to head out for chores."

"Can I help?" Sarah asked on impulse. "With the chores, I mean. I'd like to see what you do."

He looked surprised but not displeased. "Sure thing. I'm sure Caidy's got plenty of winter gear around the house that should fit you fine."

After the delicious breakfast that was more like a quiche, savory and satisfying, along with waffles Ridge made himself, Destry helped her bundle into a pair of snow pants and a parka, along with a pair of heavy boots and gloves.

She added the scarf the girl had given her and then headed out to watch the two of them deliver hay, clean out stalls, deliver feed to the River Bow horses in the barn, drive several heavy bales of hay out to various pastures for the cattle and clean out a couple of stalls.

For two hours, the work was cold and relentless, but Ridge and Destry hardly appeared to notice. They laughed together, sang a couple of silly Christmas carols and otherwise seemed to have a good time, while Sarah mostly tried not to stumble into their way.

When they finally walked back to the house, her cheeks felt chapped, her arm ached from the cold and raw emotion felt huge and unwieldy in her chest.

Seeing Ridge completely in his element left her more in love with him than ever. Both of them, really. She adored Destry. Both of them were as firmly planted in her heart as his heart was planted on this ranch.

What was she going to do? she thought grimly, as they walked into the warm, welcoming embrace of the house. She was in love with a man who would despise everything about her when he learned the secrets she had kept from him.

She had to tell him, soon. As much as it hurt, she had to tell him—and then she would have to figure out how to live with the consequences.

Chapter Twelve

When was she going to tell him?

She mulled over it all day and started to a dozen times, but the moment never seemed right. She didn't want to ruin Christmas morning. Then they were all having too much fun playing some of the games Destry got for Christmas. Then he took a nap on the sofa near the great room fireplace—under the multihued throw knitted by his daughter—and she didn't have the heart to tell him when he first woke. Then they were all busy getting ready for the family meal at his brother's house.

Now, here they were on the way to Taft and Laura's, and she hadn't been able to find the right moment. How could she ruin his family dinner? And if she did, she wouldn't have any way to leave and would be stuck in a miserable situation until he could take her back to the River Bow for her rental car.

Always look for an escape route. One of those subconscious lessons she'd learned from her father.

"Are you sure you're okay?" he said. "You seem tense."

She gave him a sidelong look. "I'm a stranger going to someone else's big family party. Wouldn't you feel a little stretched out of your social comfort zone?"

"Trust me, you won't feel like a stranger for long. Alex will probably try to pull a prank on us the minute we walk through the door. Maya will throw her arms around you and give you one of her awesome hugs to say hello then Laura and Becca will probably kidnap you and haul you into the kitchen to dig out all the dirty details of your life—and probably share way too many embarrassing details of *mine*."

It all sounded chaotic and terrifying and *wonderful*.

"You love your family, don't you?"

"Every last crazy one of them," he said promptly.

Her chest ached. She wanted this. The noisy chaos, the inquisitive relatives, the sense of belonging to something bigger than she was.

And the man who went along with it. She wanted him most of all.

Not trusting herself to speak, she gazed out at the steep, snow-covered mountains that loomed out the windshield. After a moment, he reached out and gripped her fingers in his.

"It won't be that bad. Don't worry. Everybody will love you, I promise. And if it's all too much for you, let me know and I can take you back to the River Bow."

She forced a smile, touched beyond words at his concern for her.

He squeezed her fingers. "At some point, you're going to tell me what's bothering you, right?"

Was she that obvious? She flushed. Probably. He seemed to know what she was thinking before she even realized it. "Yes," she finally murmured. "But not right now, okay?"

His expression was intense and curious, but he said nothing as they drove across a bridge and headed on a lane through towering, snow-covered evergreen trees.

Finally they pulled up in front of a beautiful two-story home constructed of honey-colored pine logs and river rock with a wraparound porch. White icicle lights dripped from the porch roof and the gables of the house. It reminded her a great deal of the River Bow ranch house, though on a smaller scale.

The scene inside played out just as Ridge predicted. It was as if he'd read the script ahead of time, she thought.

A young dark-haired boy rushed over to greet them the moment they walked through the door.

"Hey, Uncle Ridge. Shake my hand."

"Why?"

"No reason. I just want you to."

Ridge snorted, obviously up to the game, but he played along anyway and held his hand out, then pretended to jump away in shock from a little tingly joy buzzer in the boy's hand, to peals of laughter from Alex.

"Oh, you got me."

"Guess what I got from Santa Claus? A whole box of joke and magic stuff. It's so awesome!"

"Wow. I bet your mom was just thrilled at Santa Claus for that one."

"Yep. Dad thought it was *hilarious*."

"He would," Ridge answered wryly.

"Hey, Destry. Shake my hand," the boy said.

"Forget it, Alex!" she said. "You think I didn't just see you punk my dad?"

"Aw, man." With a disappointed look, Alex rushed off, probably to gear up for another trick.

Before Sarah could catch her breath, an adorable girl with Down syndrome and the sweetest smile she'd ever seen came over and hugged both Ridge and Destry, who clearly adored her.

"Maya, this is our friend Sarah. She teaches first grade, just like you're in. Sarah, this is our Maya."

"Hi," Maya said cheerfully. "I love my teacher. Her name is Miz L."

Just as Ridge predicted, she threw her arms around Sarah's waist without waiting for a response, and Sarah smiled and hugged her back, completely charmed.

The sisters-in-law didn't precisely kidnap her, but they did push her into the kitchen with firm determination, where they set her to work stirring gravy with her good hand, all while subtly and gently interrogating her.

She loved every moment of it.

She had met each of Ridge's brothers separately, but seeing them together, she would have had a tough time figuring out which twin was which if not for the adorably fat baby boy Trace held.

All of them treated her with warm acceptance. By the time they left three hours later—full of delicious food, fun conversation and more holiday spirit than she ever imagined— she felt fully enmeshed into the Bowman family.

How would she ever say goodbye to them all?

* * *

"What a great day," Destry declared when they were in the pickup truck again, prepared to head back to the River Bow. "Best. Christmas. Ever."

He grinned at his daughter. "It was pretty awesome, though I believe I remember you saying the same thing last year."

"That's because every year just gets better and better. Next year will be the best yet because Ben and Caidy will be there with Jack and Ava. I missed them all. Who knows? Maybe Caidy will even have a baby by then."

It was certainly possible, though the idea of his baby sister—the one he had practically raised since she was a teenager—becoming a mother was not a subject he wanted to think too long about.

He had his suspicions in that direction about Taft and Laura, though they hadn't said anything. Laura had a certain unmistakable glow about her, and Taft couldn't seem to keep his eyes off her—not that he ever could. His brother had loved his wife for most of their lives. Ridge loved seeing them all so happy.

In contrast to the Bowman clan, with each mile, the lovely woman beside him seemed to grow more and more quiet.

"Sorry about my crazy family," he said as they neared the River Bow. "I'm afraid they can be a little overwhelming."

She shook her head. "They were wonderful. So kind and welcoming, even though I'm a stranger. Everything was perfect. Destry is right. It was the best Christmas ever."

So why did she seem so sad? he wondered. He wanted

to ask, but the moment didn't seem right with Destry listening in from the backseat.

While she seemed to enjoy herself, he didn't miss the way she maintained a careful distance from the family. She smiled and laughed and chatted, all while keeping something of herself in reserve, as if she didn't want to let them all into her life too far.

That hadn't stopped everyone from falling for her, just like he had. Both Laura and Becca had ganged up to corner him in the kitchen and not-so-subtly dig for information about her and, he thought, to try to sniff out any romantic entanglements between the two of them.

He wanted to think he'd been sly and evasive, but judging by a certain crafty gleam in the expression worn by both of his sisters-in-law, he had a feeling he hadn't been very successful.

He glanced at Sarah again. Her broken arm was clutched to her stomach, and she seemed to be clenching and unclenching the other hand on her thigh.

He thought about what Destry had said…that the next Christmas would be even better for them. How could it possibly beat this one if Sarah wasn't there?

His heart seemed to race as the truth seeped through. He wanted her in his life permanently.

Yeah, it was early, but he had always been a man who knew what he wanted. Things hadn't worked out so well when it came to Melinda, but he knew in his heart that Sarah was different. She was sweet and kind. She loved his daughter and had seemed to enjoy his family.

He didn't know how they could make it work long-distance. With phone, email, Skype, maybe they could figure it out for the short term. He could arrange short visits to the coast, and maybe she could come back here during school vacations.

His mind raced with possibilities. What were the chances she might be willing to relocate? He couldn't leave the ranch, but maybe he could persuade her Pine Gulch had a wonderful elementary school that might be in need of a dedicated first-grade teacher. He would have to talk to the principal of the elementary school, Jenny Dalton, to see if she expected any positions to open up for the next school year....

Whoa. Slow it down, now. As they pulled up to the ranch house, he forced himself to rein in his thoughts as he would old Bob. These powerful feelings seething through him were too new, too raw. He needed time to become accustomed to them—not to mention that she seemed to be fighting this with everything she had.

They could talk later, when Destry was in bed, he vowed as they walked inside the house. They could sit by the fire again in the great room, and he would push until she told him what was bothering her.

Tri hopped to greet them first thing, wagging his tail with excitement.

"Destry, why don't you let Tri out? Then you can help me do evening chores, if you want."

"Sure," she said with that bright eagerness that always warmed his heart. He hoped she never lost that attitude, like helping her old dad feed the stock was a rare and precious treat.

"You're welcome to come down to the barn if you want," he offered to Sarah.

She still seemed subdued and didn't meet his gaze. "I think I'll pass, if you don't mind. My arm is kind of achy."

"No problem. We'll be back up to the house in an hour."

"Okay."

She gave him a smile he thought looked forced.

Yeah, they needed to have a talk. He would listen to her, would try to help with whatever bothered her and then he would tell her he was falling in love with her.

The back door opened just as she was rolling her suitcase one-handed out of her bedroom.

Her heart sank and her insides roiled. She was very afraid she would be sick—and not from the delicious meal she hadn't been able to eat much of at the Bowman family party.

If only she had been ten minutes faster, she would have been gone before they returned from the barn.

Skulking off in the darkness on Christmas night was a stupid and cowardly thing to do, but then she had spent a week being stupid and cowardly, running from this moment. Why ruin a perfect record?

Destry came in first, chattering away to her father about a horseback ride she wanted to take the next day.

She froze when she saw Sarah standing with her suitcase in her hand, stopping so abruptly her father nearly ran into her.

"Hey," Ridge said to his daughter, holding a hand to steady both of them. His gaze lifted, and he saw her and then the suitcase she pulled. For one brief instant, she saw a host of emotions she couldn't read in his gaze, ending in a fierce blaze of anger that he quickly contained.

"Going somewhere?"

She wanted to burst into tears, cover her face and

run out the door, but she had been cowardly enough for a dozen lifetimes.

She squared her shoulders. "Yes. I'm driving into Jackson for the night. I...found a hotel and arranged a flight back to California tomorrow."

Destry made a little sound of distress. "But why?" she wailed. "We were having such a great Christmas."

Her chest ached as if the girl had punched her. Oh, she hated this. "I know, honey. You've been wonderful. I've enjoyed our time together so much. I just... I have to go."

She didn't know what else to say, even as she heard how lame the words sounded.

"Why?" Ridge demanded.

For a fairly innocuous word, it sliced and clawed at her, leaving her emotions in shreds.

"I just do. I don't belong here. You've been kind enough to open your home to me, but...I don't want to overstay my welcome."

"So you're running off at 9:00 p.m. on Christmas night. That really seemed the best time to leave?"

"If you'll remember, I tried to leave a dozen times these past few days. There was always another reason why I should stay."

"And now you've run out of reasons. Is that what you're saying?"

He looked furious again, and something else, something deeper.

He looked hurt.

She thought of the kisses between them, all the unspoken feelings in her heart. More than she had wanted anything in her life—more than every dreamed-of Christmas gift thrown together—she wanted to stay here at the River Bow with him, to give these growing feelings a chance to blossom.

She knew she couldn't. He wouldn't want her here after he knew the truth—and if she was running out of anything, it was the dozens of excuses she had cowardly used to avoid exactly this moment.

"I don't belong here," she tried again, but he cut her off.

"You do and we both know it. You fit into this house—into our *lives*—perfectly."

She sucked in a breath as fresh pain jabbed her. So he sensed it, too, how *right* they could have been together, if things had been different.

Tears burned and she blinked quickly to force them back.

"I don't. I can't. If you knew the truth about me, you would agree."

"Tell me. You've been hiding something since the moment you showed up. What the hell is going on? Don't you even have the guts to tell me as you're walking out the door?"

She pressed a hand to her stomach. She had to tell him. Now. She gazed at Destry, watching the interaction with confused misery on her sweet features, and Sarah's heart broke all over again.

Ridge intercepted her look and shifted his attention to his daughter.

"Destry, will you go to your room, please?"

"But, Dad!"

"Please, Des."

Though she gave her father a mutinous look, she moved through the kitchen with the three-legged little dog hopping along behind her. Just before she left the room, she turned one more time to glare at Sarah.

"I thought we were friends. Friends don't just turn their backs on each other," she said, with all the dramatic flair of a preteen.

"I'm so sorry, Destry. I really am."

The snake-eyed look she received in return told her plainly the girl didn't believe her. She could hear Destry racing up the stairs and slamming her door hard behind her. Each sound only added to her guilt and pain.

"You want to tell me now what the hell is going on?" Ridge said. "You've been trying to run away since the moment you stepped onto the River Bow. Is it because I told you last night I was starting to have feelings for you? Because I'm falling in love with you?"

Joy burned through her, fierce and bright as a Christmas star. For a long moment, she wanted to just bask in it, then reality abruptly doused her elation. Those tears burned harder, and this time she couldn't seem to force them all back.

"You're not in love with me." Her voice sounded ragged, small. "You can't be."

He narrowed his gaze. "Hate to break it to you, sweetheart, but you don't get to decide whether I love you or not."

A tiny sound escaped—a gasp or a sob, she wasn't sure—and then another one. She had to leave soon, while she could still keep her tears contained.

"I didn't want this," she said. "I never should have come here. I'm so sorry."

"You're sorry I love you?" he asked harshly. "Or you're sorry you love me back? Whatever you think of me, I'm not stupid, Sarah. I know you have feelings for me, too."

It would be far easier to tell him he was mistaken,

that she didn't care for him at all. That she was leaving to avoid any further awkwardness between them.

She had lied all this time, but she knew she wouldn't be able to make that blatant a falsehood believable to either one of them.

"Admit it," he pressed. "You care about me, too."

She couldn't answer, could only gaze at him with her heart aching and misery pulsing through her with a heartbeat of its own.

Some of her mute distress must have showed on her features. His anger seemed to ease, and he took a step toward her, his eyes dark with concern.

"Sarah, what's going on? Just tell me. It can't be that bad. I love you. Whatever it is, we'll work it out, I swear."

"Not this," she whispered.

"Tell me."

This was the hardest thing she had ever done. She pressed her broken arm to her stomach, the cold, hard weight of the cast digging into her flesh through her clothes.

She couldn't delay anymore. She owed him an explanation, one she should have given the moment she rang the front doorbell of the River Bow.

She drew in a ragged breath through a throat that sudden burned with emotions and straightened her shoulders.

"Okay, I'll tell you," she said. "I think my brother killed your parents."

Chapter Thirteen

Ridge heard her, but somehow the words didn't seem real.

I think my brother killed your parents.

He couldn't think what to say for several long seconds, and she continued to gaze at him with sheer misery in her eyes.

"What are you talking about?"

His mouth felt numb suddenly and he could barely get the words out.

She pressed her lips together. "Sarah Whitmore hasn't always been my name. It was my mother's maiden name. Until the courts finally allowed us to legally change it when I was twelve, my name was Sarah Malikov. That's the rough translation, anyway. It's spelled completely differently, but Sarah is the English pronunciation."

"You're…Russian?"

"No. I'm American. I was born here and have lived

here all my life. My mother was, as well. My father, on the other hand, was from Moscow."

She drew in a shaky breath and seemed to press her cast farther into her stomach. "He was a *Pakhan* in a Russian *Bratva.* Basically the equivalent of a mob boss."

A mob boss. Her father? She taught first grade! How could this even be possible?

I think my brother killed your parents.

"And your…brother?" he managed.

"Followed right along in his footsteps. I told you we were all separated after the divorce. My father raised Josef—Joe—to be exactly like him."

"You said he was killed twelve years ago," he said. The forgotten half memory surged to the surface.

"He was. Twelve years ago this month, on Christmas Day."

That was only a few days after his parents died, he realized. Was there really a connection?

"He was killed in a hotel room in Boise during an argument with an associate after a criminal operation went wrong. I believe that job was the theft of your parents' art collection."

He tried to put the pieces together, but they were slippery as muddy calves and just as uncooperative.

"Why would you possibly think so? Because you found a painting in your father's things?"

She met his gaze, her blue eyes murky and dark. "Because I found *dozens* of paintings. A storage unit full of them. Your mother's work, as well as other Western artists."

She spoke in a low, emotionless voice, and he heard her words as if from a great distance, as if she were a stranger.

Apparently she was.

Dozens of paintings. It must be his parents' entire collection, or most of it, anyway. She couldn't possibly be making something like that up—but could the paintings actually have been squirreled away in a storage unit somewhere, all this time? It made sense and certainly explained why nothing much had ever turned up on the black market.

Ridge couldn't seem to think straight. His thoughts and emotions seemed to be racketing around like cats after a recalcitrant ball of string—shock, disbelief, anger. Surely it couldn't be true. Surely it was unimaginable that he and his brothers had been looking all these years for the murderers and suddenly a relative of a viable suspect just happened to show up on his doorstep.

Not just *happened to show up.* This had been planned from the beginning. She had come here on purpose. Suddenly Ridge could focus on only one thing that seemed to push away everything else—his deep, aching sense of betrayal.

"You've known. This whole time you were in my house, sleeping in my sister's room, laughing with my daughter—kissing me, damn it, letting me come to care about you—you kept this a secret."

Her mouth seemed to wobble, but she firmed it into a tight line. "Yes."

"Why?"

"I should have told you that first day. I meant to, but then I fell down your stairs and everything became so tangled."

"You still could have told me at any point in the past several days. Instead, you kept your mouth shut. This is one hell of a secret, Sarah. I can't believe this. Why didn't you say anything?"

She had known the answers to all the questions he and his siblings had been asking for a dozen years. He still couldn't seem to wrap his head around it. What if she was wrong? But why else would her father have all the paintings?

What a freaking mess.

"Why did you come here?" he demanded. "Why not just turn the paintings over to the authorities in the first place and let them handle it?"

Sarah didn't know how to answer. She couldn't tell him something had been driving her to come here, to meet the family of the woman who had painted such beautiful work. The moment she had seen those paintings, they had haunted her and then when she found out the deadly provenance, she could only think about giving them all back.

It made no sense, even to her, but it had seemed like the only thing she could do.

"I don't know," she answered, truthfully enough. "I've also asked myself how the artwork came to be in my father's possession in the first place and why he never sold it off, all these years later. Perhaps he sold a piece here or there. I won't know until your family insurance investigators go through the pieces and see if anything is missing. But whatever else anyone can say about Vasily Malikov, he was generally an astute, if absolutely amoral, businessman. He was always looking at the bottom line—so why would he hang on to everything and not sell it along the way?"

"You knew him. I didn't. You tell me."

She hadn't known him. Her father and his lifestyle had been completely foreign to her. She had *hated* visits with him. She used to suffer stomach cramps for weeks before every visit, but her mother would never have defied a court order.

"My father loved two things—my brother and vengeance."

"Vengeance."

He said the word with a grim emphasis that made her shiver.

"Yes. He lived and died by it. If someone crossed him, they paid the price. I'm positive the man who killed Joe wouldn't have made it far before my father found him and took back the stolen artwork he believed was his by rights, in his twisted way. As to why he kept it all these years, I can't say. Perhaps it was some kind of shrine to my brother or a reminder to my father of all that he had lost. Or maybe he was simply waiting until prices went up. I doubt we'll ever know."

"None of that explains why you didn't tell me the moment I answered the door that first day. You lied to me from the beginning."

"Yes," she said.

"Like father, like daughter."

Her face felt cold as blood rushed away at his deliberate cruelty. She had earned his disdain, every drop of it. That didn't make it hurt less.

"I have been trying to escape that legacy my entire life, but perhaps you're right. You understand now why I tried to warn you not to open your home to me. I knew you wouldn't want me here if you had known my family was more than likely involved somehow in your parents' murders."

"You're right about that," he snapped.

She forced herself to breathe around the pain. Her eyes watered, and the family room Christmas-tree lights through the kitchen doorway seemed to glimmer and merge.

Her beautiful Christmas—the best one ever, just as Destry said—lay in ruins like so much torn and tattered wrapping paper.

The season of hope and forgiveness was lovely in the abstract. In reality, it could be just as flimsy and insubstantial as that paper.

"You see now why I was leaving. I knew you would h-hate me when you found out." Despite all her best efforts, her voice wobbled and she had to fight down a sob again. "I'm sorry I didn't tell you. After I broke my arm, everything was so tangled, and by the time I could sort it all out, I already cared about you and Destry so much. I'm sorry to hurt you. So sorry, Ridge. I…thank you for everything. Please tell Destry—all your family—that I'm sorry. My attorney will be in touch."

"Why?"

She gripped her suitcase so hard her fingers felt as if they were fused into the handle. "So I can return the rest of the paintings to you, of course. Why else?"

She didn't think she had room for any more pain, but the shock in his eyes proved her wrong. "Really, Ridge? You honestly think so poorly of me that you think I would keep stolen property?"

He didn't answer, and another arrow found its way home.

"I suppose I can't blame you," she managed through the last of her strength. "As you said, I'm my father's daughter. I hope you can someday see I'm my own person before I am Vasily Malikov's child."

She turned and headed for the door and her rental car. She almost made it outside before he yanked her suitcase away. For one wild, breathless moment she thought he was going to carry it back inside for her.

I love you. Whatever it is, we'll work it out, I swear.

No. Instead, he stiffly walked to her rental car, opened the trunk and shoved the suitcase in.

He held the driver's door open for her. Furious as he was at her, the hard, implacable, *completely wonderful* man held the door open and even helped her inside the car. Then he backed away and stood outside on an ice-cold Christmas night without his coat, arms at his side as he watched her back the rental car out, turn it around and head down the road.

Only after she was certain he couldn't see her did the tears finally burst through.

"You want to tell us what's going on?"

Ridge looked up from his work to find his annoying-as-hell brothers watching him with matching frowns.

"I'm cleaning out the stalls," he growled. "Why don't you grab a couple of shovels and help instead of standing there with your thumbs up your asses?"

Taft raised an eyebrow at Trace before turning back to him.

"You seem to be doing a fine job. Judging by that little remark, I'd say shoveling, er, Shinola is just what you need to be doing right now."

After a sleepless night, he had been up as early as he could, looking for any kind of physical labor to hold back the pain.

"You two don't have anything better to do than come down here and make stupid comments?"

"Not really," Trace said.

"Speak for yourself," Taft muttered. "The kids stayed at their grandma Pendleton's last night. I could be sleeping in with my lovely wife right now. Or not sleeping in."

"So why are you here?" he demanded.

Again, they exchanged looks that made him want to punch one or both of them. In his current mood, he was pretty sure he could take them both without working up much of a sweat.

"Apparently Gabi received a rather frantic call from Destry this morning that Sarah left and now you've gone mental."

He kept shoveling, barely looking up at them. Maybe if he worked hard enough, this ache in his chest would ease. "Did she?"

"Is it true you took down all the Christmas decorations in the middle of the night?" Trace asked.

He let out a huffing sort of sigh. Okay, that *had* been a little mental, a crazy impulse he couldn't really explain. One minute, he'd been sitting by the fire and looking at the Christmas tree, the next, he'd been pulling off ornaments.

"Not everything. Just the big tree in the great room and the garlands. There's still plenty of Christmas crap all over the house. It had to come down sometime, didn't it?"

He shoveled harder, avoiding their gazes and the concern he didn't want to see.

"Why did Sarah leave?" Trace asked, in the same kind of overly solicitous voice a police chief would probably have to use when dealing with people who needed a seventy-two hour hold or something. "Did you two have a fight?"

His whole body ached as if both brothers had taken turns pummeling him. He didn't know how the hell he would ever get past it. "You could say that," he muttered.

"It must have been a pretty good one if you were taking down your Christmas tree at two in the morning on December 26," Trace observed.

He wasn't obliged to explain any of his actions to his younger brothers, so he opted not to answer.

"What did you do to her?" Taft pressed.

He stopped shoveling and gave a steely glare that encompassed both of them. "What makes you think I did anything?"

"Just a wild guess," Taft said. "I thought she seemed really sweet. Laura loved her and kept saying how perfect she was for you."

"I had the same conversation with Becca," Trace offered.

He gritted his teeth as if it took all his force of will and reminded himself it would be juvenile to "accidentally" let a little shit fly on both of his brothers.

"You both misunderstood," he said calmly. "She was a guest in my home. That's all."

A guest there under false pretenses, he wanted to add.

"That doesn't quite explain why you took down your Christmas tree in the middle of the night and have been shoveling out the stalls since before sunrise," Taft drawled.

He wanted to tell them it was none of their damn business, but that would have been a lie. They needed to know about Sarah's deception and her family history. He had to tell them, but didn't know how. He was ridiculously aware that after everything, part of the reason for his hesitation was a reluctance for them to think poorly of her.

He was suddenly exhausted, so tired he couldn't think straight. He leaned against the half wall of the stall, the handle of the shovel loose in his hand.

"She's gone."

"That's what Destry said," Trace said. "She told Gabi that Sarah came home right after our party and packed up her things."

"I don't get it," Taft said, with more compassion than he would have given his former hell-raising brother credit for. "She seemed to be enjoying herself well enough. We all thought she was great. Was it something we all said?"

Ridge took off his leather glove and rubbed at his face.

"No. I guess her conscience just caught up with her, and she was tired of the lies."

"What did she lie about?" Trace asked.

Damn, he didn't want to do this. He needed air suddenly. Air and sunlight and the pure crystalline beauty of a cold December morning on his ranch.

He grabbed his Stetson from the hook where he'd hung it, shoved it on and walked outside. After a moment the twins followed.

"What's going on?" Taft demanded.

"You know that painting she brought, the one Mom did of Caidy?"

"Yes," Trace said, his tone wary.

"Apparently, she's got plenty more where that came from. A whole storage unit full of stolen artwork from the famous Bowman Western art collection."

His brothers both stared at him, and he was aware of a horse whinnying somewhere, of the cold puffs of air they were all breathing out, of the hard knot that had lodged in his chest sometime in the past twelve hours and didn't show any sign of easing.

Taft was the first to break the silence. "Sorry. She has what?"

"She has more artwork from the collection. Dozens of items. She doesn't know if it's complete or not but it's in a storage unit somewhere belonging to her father, where it's apparently been since the murders."

"Her father—" Trace began.

"Was a Russian mafia boss whose only son was apparently killed days after the murders just a few hours from here. Sarah doesn't think it's a coincidence. For the record, neither do I."

His brothers stared.

"You're saying Sarah's father and brother were involved in the murders?" Trace finally asked. His eyes had that flinty look Ridge recognized. Sometimes he forgot what a damn good cop his brother was.

"The father, I don't know. The brother, most definitely. He was murdered in Boise a few days after the murders. Sarah's theory is, her brother fought with a partner who killed him, then her father took vengeance for his son's murder and ended up with the artwork. Why he kept it all is a mystery to her. She was estranged from the man and stumbled onto the storage unit while taking care of his affairs after his death."

He couldn't look at either of his brothers, wary at what their reaction must be. Taft had welcomed Sarah into his home. She had played with all their children, had held Trace's baby, had chatted with their wives—all while keeping this huge secret. He still couldn't quite wrap his head around it all.

"She told you all this last night before she left?" Trace asked. Some of the hardness of his features seemed to have eased.

"Yeah. Not until last night. She was here for days without saying a word. She should have told me when she first showed up at the ranch. She stayed here under false pretenses."

"The way I remember it, she stayed here because you insisted," Taft pointed out. Ridge actually formed a fist and barely refrained from letting it swing—he couldn't deny the truth of what his brother said.

"I guess that makes me the idiot, doesn't it?"

"Is that why you're mad at her?" Trace asked after a pause. "Because she didn't tell you her family might have been involved in Mom and Dad's deaths?"

Mad was a mild word for this chaos of emotions broiling under his skin. "Isn't that enough?"

"Just wondering. How old is Sarah?" Trace asked. "I'm guessing around Caidy's age, right?"

"Give or take a year or so."

"So she would have been, what, sixteen, seventeen?"

He narrowed his gaze. "Yeah. And your point?"

"Do you think she had anything to do with the murders?"

He stared. "No. Of course not! She was estranged from her father most of her life. She barely knew the man, and she certainly wasn't some big art thief."

Trace shrugged. "In that case, feel free to correct me if I'm wrong, but it seems to me you're not just an idiot. You're a *stupid* idiot."

He ground his teeth and drew that fist again. "You want to put some muscle behind that, baby brother?"

"Don't be an even bigger ass," Trace said. "Tough as you are, you can't take on both of us."

"Don't drag me into this," Taft protested. "I'm just along for the ride."

What was he doing? He wasn't going to fight with his brothers, as angry as he was at the world in general. Ridge raked a hand through his hair and realized he was suddenly freaking cold.

Why the hell were they standing outside? Oh, right. He had walked out first. He felt as if he had been in a daze since the moment he had walked into the house the night before and found Sarah holding her suitcase.

"She lied to me. That's what bothers me. Or at least she neglected to mention something pretty damn important. She stayed in my house, she hung out with my daughter, she spent Christmas with all of us, for crying out loud."

She made me love her.

Trace raised an eyebrow. "So?"

"So the whole time, she knew her family had been involved in destroying ours."

"She brought us Mom's painting, though," Taft pointed out. "She didn't have to do that. She could have just stayed quiet about the whole thing, and nobody would have known. That says something about her, doesn't it?"

He sighed. "She said she's going to have her attorney work with the authorities to catalog what's there and return the whole collection to us."

His announcement was met with a long, echoing silence, and both brothers looked at him with the same astounded expression.

"Man, I hate to say this, but Trace is right," Taft finally said. "You are one stupid idiot. And an ass, to boot. So she didn't tell you the truth. Sounds to me like she's intending to do the right thing now. Or do you think she's lying about giving back the collection?"

He shook his head. "No! Of course not. If she says she'll do it, she will. I trust her word."

The brothers looked at each other. Taft was the first to snicker, but Trace wasn't far behind.

"Wait. Let me get this straight," Trace said. "You're saying you trust the word of a woman who has spent the past several days lying to you?"

Ridge closed his eyes, feeling the pale sunlight on his face as he pondered the ridiculousness of his own words. She had lied to him about her father, her brother. She hadn't told him about the paintings.

He had no reason to trust that she was telling the truth now, but somehow he couldn't make himself believe otherwise.

"Yeah. Yeah, I do. I believe she fully plans to give us back the rest of the paintings. She had no reason to lie about that part, did she?"

"So you don't think Sarah had anything to do with the murders and you believe she's going to give us back the paintings she found. You trust her word. Explain to me again the part that has you pissed off enough to take down the decorations on an eighteen-foot Christmas tree by yourself last night?"

As he listened to Trace's completely reasonable question, that hard knot in his chest seemed to jiggle a little. It didn't quite break free, but it was close.

"Because I'm an ass," he murmured.

"No," Taft said cheerfully. "You're just in love. Welcome to the club, dude. It makes you do all kinds of crazy things."

"Like jump in a river to save your ex-fiancee's children." Trace jabbed at his twin.

"Or give up a decade-long quest for justice and vengeance in order to protect a young girl's future," Taft countered.

"Looks like I made the right choice on that one," Trace said. "Thanks to Sarah, we might find all those answers anyway."

Trace was right. Ridge rubbed a hand over his eyes, exhausted all over again. She had brought them more than a painting their mother had created—even more than the dozens of stolen art pieces that might eventually find their way back to the River Bow.

She had brought them the chance to find answers to the questions that had haunted them all.

She didn't have to come in person to deliver the painting. She could have made a phone call. *Oh, by the way, I think I have something that might be yours.* Or she could have handled the whole thing through attorneys.

Or she could have kept the artwork and sold it piece by piece on the black market and made a freaking fortune.

She had done none of those things. Instead, she had taken a plane a thousand miles, had rented a car, then had driven out to the River Bow to speak with Margaret and Frank Bowman's descendants in person. She had shown amazing courage and strength of character.

He claimed he loved her but at the first bit of difficulty, he had shoved her away, said horrible things to her. He had carried her lousy suitcase out to the car, for heaven's sake.

He wanted a do-over for the entire past twelve hours.

He opened his eyes to find both of his brothers looking at him with amused, indulgent expressions.

"What the hell am I supposed to do now?"

Taft shrugged. "If it were me, I'd already be in my truck going after her."

"Same goes," Trace said.

He didn't know where she had gone, other than Jackson to stay the night then she was catching a flight out today. He didn't have the first idea how to find her and decided his best bet was to call in reinforcements.

He headed for the house. "Trace, now you've got something to work with. Go do your cop thing. You should be able to track down the brother, Josef Malikov, son of Vasily Malikov, who was some kind of mob boss. See if you can find out details of what happened to him, then look for any known associates who might have disappeared around the same time. Sarah thinks the two fought, and her brother was killed in the process. She also believes her father probably had the man offed who killed his son. Let's see what else we can discover."

"What can I do?" Taft asked.

"Keep your fingers crossed that I can find her. And that she'll find it in her heart to forgive me when I do."

Sarah sat in the café of her hotel, moving her spoon aimlessly through the oatmeal she had ordered but couldn't eat, lifting up her coffee cup then setting it back down again without a sip, leafing through a magazine without registering a single word on the pages.

She was a mess. Plain and simple.

Trying to sleep had been an abject failure. Apparently, eating wasn't something she was up to handling today, either.

The busy hotel bustled with people, families eating together or couples wearing what looked like expensive matching skiwear.

Jackson Hole was packed at Christmastime. She should have expected people would flock here to ski for the holidays. Finding a room had been a challenge, and she had ended up with one that would normally have been way out of her budget.

She could have just driven around in the rental car all night for all the sleep she ended up getting in that pricey hotel bed.

Her flight didn't leave for hours. How would she possibly fill that time? She didn't feel like shopping on this busy day-after-Christmas return day. It made no sense to pay extra for late checkout at the hotel, only to stare at a TV showing programs she didn't care about.

Since she still had the rental car, perhaps she should just take a drive through the raw wintry splendor of the Tetons. She took a sip of her coffee—an actual sip this time—trying to summon the energy to do anything.

All she really wanted to do was curl up in a ball and weep for days, but that wouldn't accomplish anything.

She felt more bruised and battered than the day she fell down the stairs at the River Bow, as if every muscle and sinew had been stretched to the breaking point.

She deserved the pain and more. A little honesty on her part would have prevented this whole thing. If she had told him that very first day why she had come to the River Bow, she never would have been in this situation. She wouldn't have fallen in love with the man and wouldn't now be consumed with the pain of losing him before she had ever really known the joy of being in love with a good man.

A laughing couple came in with a girl about Destry's age, dressed in cute brown snow pants and a pink parka that would have looked adorable on Des. She watched them interact for a moment until the pain became too much.

She had loved Destry as much as she loved the girl's father. Her heart felt shattered, knowing she had left without saying a proper goodbye to her.

She sat for a few moments more, until watching the laughing father, mother, girl became too tired for her then she signed the bill with a healthy tip and left the restaurant to return to her room.

There was no sense staying here. She would drive around for a while, perhaps make a stop at the elk refuge on the edge of Grand Teton National Park then head for the airport.

Packing the few things she had used from her suitcase overnight took her all of five minutes. When she finished, she took the elevator down to the lobby and handed her keys back to the polite desk clerks.

Just as she turned away, she caught sight of a tall man in a cowboy hat charging through the door, and her heartbeat kicked up a notch.

Settle down, she ordered herself. Tall cowboys in Jackson Hole weren't exactly an endangered species. She reached for the handle of her suitcase and started for the door when that particular cowboy shifted in her direction and she froze as if he had tossed her out into the snow.

Her heart began to pound and nerves twirled in her

stomach. How had he found her? She hadn't told him
where she was staying, had she?

More importantly, *why* was he here? Had he come
to fight with her more, to inform her how wrong she
was to have kept the truth from him as long as she had?

Like father, like daughter.

The words were seared into her psyche. She drew in
a shaky breath. She couldn't do this. Not here, in this
bustling lobby. She wasn't strong enough to face him,
not after she had been sobbing all night and probably
looked a mess.

He hadn't seen her yet. Instead, he was heading to
the front desk she had just left, probably looking for
her room number—unless this was all a horrible coincidence, which she sincerely doubted.

She considered her options, none of them very appealing. The best of the lot was to avoid the situation entirely
and sneak out a different way, without him spying her.

Just then, a large family carrying snowboards and
skis tromped through the lobby in heavy ski boots. She
slipped into step beside them, trying to blend as they all
crossed the lobby together.

The strategy almost worked. Unfortunately they were
heading to the front, probably catching one of the ski re-
sort shuttles, while she needed to go to the parking lot.

Just as she turned to take different doors, she heard
a deep, focused, wonderfully familiar voice. "Sarah."

Shoot.

With a few more pithy words racketing around in her
brain, she forced herself to turn slowly, hating this, hating her father and Joe for leaving her this legacy of pain
to deal with. Even hating Ridge a little for being so wonderful that she couldn't help but fall in love with him.

"Ridge," she said in a feigned tone of surprise. "What are you doing here?"

"You left your scarf."

He held up the soft knitted gift Destry had given her. Somehow it must have slipped off on her way out the door. The night before when she realized she didn't have it, she had sobbed more tears than she thought she possessed.

Her stomach fluttered at the sight of the sweet little scarf in his big, callused, outstretched hand.

"Thank you," she said. She reached for it, taking care that their fingers wouldn't brush, then tucked it into her pocket. "I wondered what happened to it."

"I found it on the sidewalk this morning. It must have fallen when you were on your way to the car."

"Ah. It was very nice of you to return it."

He looked so wonderful to her, all chiseled angles and hard edges, with his mouth set in an unsmiling line and those beautiful green eyes watching her with an expression she couldn't read. Why was he here? Why had he come all this way?

"How did you find me?"

Even as she asked the question, the answer seemed unimportant in light of her pounding heart. Emotions pressed in, heavy and suffocating. She loved him so much she couldn't breathe around it.

"I put Destry on it. It wasn't that tough, if you want the truth. You left the number of the hotel on a paper Destry found in your room. She did a reverse lookup on the computer, and when it came back to this hotel, I... took a chance."

Simply to return her scarf? Somehow she didn't think so.

"Thank you. It means a great deal to me. When I returned to San Diego, I would have missed it."

"What about us? Destry and me. Would you have missed us, too?"

She met his gaze. She couldn't seem to catch a breath suddenly, as if she had just jumped from the ski lift onto a black diamond run she couldn't handle.

"Don't do this, Ridge," she whispered. "Please, don't."

"Do what?"

"Make everything worse. I'm sorry again that I didn't tell you about my father and about Joe. You deserved to know, and I was wrong to keep that information from you, no matter my reasons."

"Yeah. You should have told me."

She tried not to reel all over again. Somehow she was able to keep control over her emotions.

"Well, okay. Now that we have that out of the way, I should go. I have a plane to catch."

"Not for five hours," he countered. "Destry also went online and figured out the only flight from Jackson to San Diego doesn't leave until later this afternoon."

"She's quite the clever little detective, isn't she?"

"When she has to be. She doesn't want to lose you, either."

That single word caught her heart like a butterfly net. She jerked her gaze up at him and desperately wished she could read more in that glittery green gaze.

"E-either?"

He gave her one of his slow, beautiful smiles that sent her pulse skyrocketing. "She wanted to come with me. She wasn't at all happy when I dropped her off to hang out with Gabi. I finally had to tell her there were certain things a man just has to do without any help from his eleven-year-old daughter."

She couldn't seem to swallow past the lump in her throat. "Like what?"

"Like grovel to the woman he loves."

She again caught on a single word. *Loves.* Not *loved.* Not *used to love.*

Loves.

Heedless of the busy lobby and the other guests bustling around them, she could only stare at him. Now she could read his expression—fierce, warm, tender.

She allowed herself to bask it in, only for a moment then did her best to force herself to focus on sense. This couldn't be happening. She didn't deserve for him to look at her like that.

"Ridge—"

"I took down the Christmas tree last night."

The non sequitur threw her. "You...did?"

"I couldn't look at it anymore. All those glittery ornaments, the garland, the lights. It hurt too much to see that huge symbol of joy in my house when I was feeling anything but happy."

"Oh."

"So this morning Des got freaked out when she woke up and found it like that, so she called Gabi, who enlisted Trace, who called Taft. My two brothers ambushed me this morning. They called me any number of names, not least of which was a stupid idiot for letting you go."

She frowned. "Did you tell them? About Joe and my father and the paintings?"

"Yeah. For the record, I gave them all that information *before* they told me in no uncertain terms that I needed to haul my ass here and bring you back."

"They said that, knowing everything?"

He nodded, reaching for her hand. Her heart was going to pound out of her chest. She couldn't seem to grasp a thought in her head through the mingled sorrow and joy of seeing him again.

"I love my brothers," he said simply. "They drive me absolutely crazy sometimes—what else are families for, right?—but they're generally both wise men who apparently have a much smarter perspective on this issue than I did."

"But I lied to you. I don't blame you for being furious with me."

"I was. Last night. This morning, I have a little more clarity. Trace wisely pointed out that you were just a girl when this all happened and that you barely knew your father or your brother. It's completely unfair to blame you for what happened to my parents. I certainly wouldn't want anybody blaming Destry for the poor decisions I've made in my life."

"The murder of your parents was far from just a poor decision," she protested.

"True. And it wasn't your fault, either."

He lifted her fingers to his mouth, this big, rough rancher, in an act of incredible tenderness that rocked her to the core.

"I love you, Sarah. I wasn't looking for it and sure as hell didn't expect it to show up on my doorstep one December morning, but there it is. I love you. I love your patience with my daughter, I love the comfort I find sitting beside you on a cold winter's night, I love that smile of yours that makes everything seem easier. I know we haven't known each other long, and we still have a lot to discover about each other, but I wanted you to know my feelings before you left. It only seemed right that we have no more secrets between us."

How could she believe him? Did she dare take a chance.

Yes.

She loved him. These few days had been magical, and she selfishly wanted more.

Joy burst through her like exploding Christmas bulbs, so bright and pure she couldn't contain it, and she smiled at him with all the tenderness spilling over inside her.

"In that case, I should probably tell you one more thing."

"What's that?" he asked.

"I love you, Ridge. I love the way you are with Destry, I love watching you care for your ranch, I love how you watch out for your neighbors. You're the hardest-working man I've ever met, but I love seeing you have fun with your family, too. I love you. I've never felt this way about anyone."

At her words, he grinned slowly, green eyes blazing. "That's the best Christmas gift anybody's ever given me, even if it is a day late."

He stepped forward. Right there in the lobby, he bent down and kissed her softly, sweetly, with an aching tenderness that made those tears start all over again.

She didn't know how she could swing so abruptly from despair to this bright glowing happiness in a matter of moments, but it didn't matter. The only important thing in her life was this man, this moment. And the miraculous joy she had found in the place she least expected it.

Epilogue

Ridge stood in front of the River Bow fireplace in his Western-cut tuxedo, anticipation and happiness bubbling through him like the champagne chilling in the kitchen being readied for all the toasts that would be made on his and Sarah's behalf in a little while.

"How are you holding up?" Taft asked the question from beside him, dressed in his own tuxedo.

Ridge hadn't been able to choose between the twins as best man so they had ended up drawing straws. Taft had ended up with this duty, but Trace hadn't complained, saying he definitely got the better end of the stick.

"Good. Great. It's a fabulous day, right? One I'll remember the rest of my life, I know. But to be honest, at this moment I just want it to be over."

His brother grinned. "Oh, how I remember that feeling. Just keep in mind, it won't be over. All the fun stuff is just beginning, right? That's probably what I'm sup-posed to say, anyway, being the best man and all that. The house looks great, by the way."

Ridge looked around at the festively decorated house. All the women he loved had outdone themselves making the place glow for the holidays. Destry and Sarah—with help from Caidy, Laura, Becca, Gabi, Ava and sweet lit-tle Maya along with Sarah's best friend from San Diego, Nicki—had been working for several days to decorate for this.

Though Thanksgiving was still a week away, his beautiful Sarah had insisted on a Christmas theme for their wedding and the result was a fairyland of lights and ornaments, ribbons and garlands.

It was a warm, welcoming place for a wedding—in no small part because of the splendid paintings that had been rehung in places of honor throughout the house.

After much discussion, he and his siblings had all picked several of their favorites from their mother's work and then had permanently lent the rest—along with the artwork of other Western artists she had col-lected through the years—to the small art museum in Pine Gulch, which would keep them on special rotating display so others could enjoy them, too.

It had been the right decision, though not an easy one.

Ridge shifted, as the music played softly and every-one waited for the bride to appear.

What a year this had been, filled with more happiness than he ever believed possible. Somehow he and Sarah had managed to work out the long-distance thing with video chats, lengthy phone calls that lasted long into the night and as many back-and-forth visits as they could manage with their schedules.

When her school contract ended in June, she had moved into an apartment in Pine Gulch, taking a summer job tutoring and signing a contract that started in the fall to teach at the elementary school.

The summer had been wonderful, filled with moonlit horseback rides, fishing trips with Destry, long, laughter-filled talks as Sarah helped him with chores around the ranch.

She merged perfectly into all their lives.

He had worried that Caidy, in particular, would take a long time to come around to her. His sister had suffered more than the rest of them at their parents' murder, since she had been there at the time and had seen the whole thing, and he had been worried she would never be able to accept the sister of the man who had killed their parents.

Their relationship had been strained at first. Then Trace had shown Caidy photographs of the two men they now knew had planned and carried out the heist that had turned into a murder—Sarah's brother, Joe, and an associate of her father's organization named Carl Bair.

Caidy—the only living eyewitness to the crimes—had immediately pointed to Bair's photograph and tearfully said he was the one who had killed both parents after Frank came at him with a shotgun, while Joe, Sarah's brother, had tried to stop him.

From the information Trace gleaned from Becca's mother a few years earlier, they knew the job was never supposed to have been violent. The thieves were expecting an empty house. Only unforeseen circumstances had led to Frank, Margaret and Caidy being there instead of at Caidy's choir concert.

The way Trace figured it, the two had fought after

the job went so horribly wrong, and Bair ended up killing Joe.

Just as Sarah predicted, Bair disappeared right after the murder, probably killed by someone else in Vasily's organization acting on his orders.

Caidy and Sarah had both cried in each other's arms at the family meeting where Trace strung together all the bits of evidence he had collected—and his sister and the woman he loved had been best of friends ever since.

Ridge knew it was a huge relief to Sarah to know that while her brother had certainly been an accessory to the murders, he hadn't pulled the trigger and had actually tried to call off Bair from killing their mother.

He pushed away thoughts of sorrow and loss as the small string orchestra softly played chamber music. This was his wedding day, and he wanted only happiness in his heart.

Finally, when he didn't think he could stand another moment of anticipation, the orchestra switched to "Ode to Joy," the song Sarah had chosen as her bridal song. He looked up to the top of the staircase, and there she was, stunning and delicate, ethereal as any Christmas angel.

His heart swelled in his chest until he couldn't breathe around the emotions.

She stood next to Trace, who felt he had won the place of honor by having the privilege of giving her away.

Ridge glanced at Destry, who looked up the stairs with her hands clasped to her chest and a dreamy expression on her freckled little face, as if she'd just been granted her dearest Christmas wish.

As Sarah walked down the stairs—those stairs that had started it all—past the beautiful framed art his mother had created, his stomach suddenly jumped with unexpected nerves.

He had failed at this once. What made him think he could do it right this time? He was impatient and could be inflexible. He liked things his way, as any of his siblings could have told her.

What if he was just a lousy husband and ended up making her miserable?

Suddenly, the highlighted words in that chapter of Luke came back to his memory, as if offered as a calming gift from the father he had loved and admired so much.

Fear not.

The words steadied him, and he smiled even as heavy emotion burned in his throat. This was right and perfect. He loved Sarah and considered her the most precious gift a man could have.

He wasn't afraid.

He only had room in his heart now for joy.

* * * * *

*Romance is the last thing on new mother
Stacey Fortune Jones's mind…until rancher Colton Foster
comes along. Will love emerge where she least expects it?*

***

"What are you thinking?" he asked.

She told herself to get over her self-consciousness. After all, this was Colton. He might as well be one of her brothers. "If you must know, Mr. Nosy, I was thinking that you have the longest eyelashes I've ever seen on a man. A lot of women would give their eyeteeth for your eyelashes."

Surprise flashed through his eyes and he laughed. It was a strong, masculine, happy sound that made her smile. "That's a first."

"No one else has ever told you that?" she asked, and narrowed her eyes in disbelief. Although Colton wasn't one to talk about his romantic life, she knew he'd spent time with more than a woman or two.

He shrugged. "The ladies usually give me other kinds of compliments," he said in a low voice.

Surprise and something else rushed through Stacey. She had never thought of Colton in those terms, and she wasn't now, she told herself. "What kinds of compliments?" she couldn't resist asking.

"Oh, this and that."

Another nonanswer, she thought, her curiosity piqued.

The song drew to a close and the bandleader tapped on his

microphone. "Ladies and gentlemen, we have less than a minute left to this year. It's time for the countdown."

Stacey absently accepted a noisemaker from a server and looked around for her daughter. "I wonder if Piper is still with Mama," she murmured, and then caught sight of her mother holding a noisemaker for the baby.

"Five…four…three…two…one," the bandleader said. "Happy New Year!"

Stacey met Colton's gaze while many couples kissed to welcome the New Year, and she felt a twist of self-consciousness. Maybe a hug would do.

Colton gave a shrug. "May as well join the crowd," he said, and lowered his head and kissed her. The sensation of the kiss sent a ripple of electricity throughout her body.

What in the world? she thought, staring up at him as he met her gaze.

"Happy New Year, Stacey."

***

Enjoy this sneak peek from
USA TODAY *bestselling author Leanne Banks's*
HAPPY NEW YEAR, BABY FORTUNE!,
the first book in
The Fortunes of Texas: Welcome to Horseback Hollow,
a brand-new six-book continuity
launching in January 2014!

SPECIAL EDITION

Life, Love and Family

Be sure to check out the first book in this year's
BRIDE MOUNTAIN miniseries
by bestselling author Gina Wilkins

A workaholic wedding planner meets a travel writer,
and soon love is in the air at
Bride Mountain, Virginia's most exciting
venue for destination weddings.

Romance is the *last* thing on the once-burned
wedding planner's mind…until a footloose travel
writer shows up, throwing her schedule—and
guarded heart—into chaos. It will take a local legend
and a passionate kiss under a bridal moon for two
total opposites to realize they could be meant for
each other.…

**Look for *MATCHED BY MOONLIGHT*
next month from Harlequin Special Edition,
wherever books are sold.**